Highlander Unleashed

by

Cynthia Breeding

Ghosts of Culloden, Book 1

Highlander Unleashed

Contact Information: info@thewildrosepress.com

Cover Art by *The Wild Rose Press, Inc.*

The Wild Rose Press, Inc.
PO Box 708
Adams Basin, NY 14410-0708
Visit us at www.thewildrosepress.com

Publishing History
First Edition, 2024
Trade Paperback ISBN 978-1-5092-5495-8
Digital ISBN 978-1-5092-5496-5

Ghosts of Culloden, Book 1
Published in the United States of America

Foreword

The Scottish New Year's Eve festival of "Hogmanay" has its roots in ancient Celtic and Norse lore. Sturdy sticks (hogmanaies) up to ten feet in length were wrapped in animal hide, ignited, and paraded around the town square at midnight. The smoke was believed to ward off evil for the coming year. The torches were then thrown into a river and the townspeople would gather in a large circle dance which often ended in embracing couples hieing to the nearest place of privacy.

Another tradition was that of "first-footing," which meant the first person to set foot in another person's home after midnight with a gift—mostly whisky—would bring good luck to the inhabitants. Highland hospitality always welcomed strangers and, in the case of first-footing, preferably dark-haired men (who were the anecdote to the blond, marauding Viking invaders of auld) would be the first-footers. and thus offer protection to the family within.

And so the legend of dark-haired male strangers begins…

Prologue

New Year's Eve: Present Day
Inverness, Scotland

Charlotte Campbell smoothed the sleeves of her leine and adjusted the airisaidh over her shoulders to provide warmth against the chill of the night air. Scotland was much colder than Texas.

"It's a good thing these costumes are made of wool," she said. "Do you think it might snow? It smells like it."

Her friend Vi snorted. "You can't *smell* snow."

"I can."

"Only because you're a romance writer. You're always making things up."

"Actually, you can smell snow." Their other friend, Thea, intervened. "If it's not freezing at ground level, falling snowflakes will begin to melt, which creates evaporative cooling, cleansing the atmosphere and making it feel—"

"Okay!" Vi laughingly held up a hand. "No lectures! You promised you'd just enjoy yourself tonight."

"I *am*." Thea smiled. "I like explaining the science of things."

Vi shook her head. "You'll have to put that aside for now. Hogmanay doesn't exactly have its roots in logic."

"That's true, Thea." Charlotte looked around at the people gathered on Castle Road, holding lit torches high.

They'd just completed a somewhat circulatory route around the base of the cliff that held the castle at its top. There had been some Gaelic chanting along the way that she didn't understand but was pretty sure was meant to ward off evil…or at least bring good luck.

There was also the myth of a dark-headed man bringing good luck, but she'd better not mention that because Vi would just accuse her of getting all romantic about legends. Still, a dark-haired stranger *did* sound interesting. Charlotte glanced around the crowd closest to her. Some of the men wore traditional bonnets with their kilts, others were bare-headed, but she saw no one fitting her imaginary description of tall, dark, and handsome. She gave herself a little shake. Maybe she *was* just a bit too romantic…

Vi gave her an appraising look. "What was that for?"

"Nothing. Just cold." Charlotte wrapped the tartan closer for emphasis. "We need to come back in the summer when it's warm."

"That's a good idea," Thea said. "We can do the Jacobite summer cruise on River Ness then."

"Isn't Nessie supposed to be in the loch?" Vi teased.

Thea blinked. "I was thinking about Culloden. Scotland lost its independence on that battlefield because they supported Bonnie Prince Charlie. So many Scots were killed."

"I know." Vi sobered. "I'm the one doing the research project for TU on eighteenth-century warfare, remember?"

Thea frowned, then straightened her brow. "I'd forgotten. It's an unusual subject—"

"Please don't say 'for a woman,' " Vi interrupted.

"You know how I feel about that."

"Rest assured. You're our Amazon." Charlotte smiled impishly. "Maybe I should say Boudicca, since she was a Celtic warrior queen and we are in Britain."

"Yes! That would be perfect! There's even a statue of her in her chariot by Westminster Bridge in London," Thea added, not looking in the least disturbed by Vi's outburst.

Charlotte smiled to herself. It was a good thing they'd all known each other since grade school, but it was still a wonder the three of them were friends since they were so different. Thea—Athena—was a thinker and Vi—Vihansa—was a doer and she…well, she tended to go off into flights of fancy.

Like looking for that dark-haired stranger. Inspiration for her next book. She looked around the crowd, which was now throwing the lit torches into the River Ness in anticipation of starting the circle dance which would end the public festivities. For a moment, she thought she'd spotted a black-haired man at the edge of the crowd. He looked more rugged, more muscular than the men milling around. Then, in a swirl of muted plaid, he turned and was gone.

Charlotte squinted. Gone? He'd just been there. He couldn't have disappeared.

Vi's voice brought her back to her friends.

"Yes, well." Vi sounded somewhat mollified after being compared to a warrior queen.

"I think the dance is getting started," Thea said.

"We didn't get these costumes just to stand around and watch. Let's join up." Charlotte replied just as a man approached to ask a question.

Vi waved them on and stayed to answer him.

Charlotte and Thea had just started toward the dancers when Thea stopped suddenly.

She pointed. "I just saw a man fall down over there."

"Probably drunk. It's pretty common tonight." Charlotte laughed.. "Come on."

"You go. I'm going to make sure he isn't hurt," Thea replied.

Charlotte knew from past experience that Thea always had a soft spot for the down and out—although she hadn't meant the thought to be a pun—so there was no point in arguing. She nodded and continued on.

In a short time, she'd joined hands with the other revelers and was skipping in a somewhat convoluted circle—thanks to whisky having been consumed with the previous proceedings—along the banks of the river and into the street.

Some of the dancers broke rank, led by a young woman whose long, auburn hair swirled around her as she formed an inner circle that moved counter to the outer one. When Charlotte reached out to join hands again, she found herself looking into the eyes of the dark stranger she'd seen earlier.

Close up, he was even taller than she'd thought. His hand was warm and strong as it grasped hers, and he grinned, showing a dimple on one cheek. He didn't speak, but the speed of the dance had picked up so much that Charlotte would have had trouble answering him if he had.

Finally, the pace slowed and the merrymakers launched into an edition of *Auld Lang Syne.* And as the final lyrics were sung, he leaned over.

"Would ye be mindin' if I stole a kiss, lass?" He grinned again. "'Tis tradition."

Would she mind? Mind? *Mind*? Charlotte had a hard time not throwing herself at him. What a perfect way to end Hogmanay! And the man even had a Scottish burr!

"Aye," she replied, trying to mimic his accent. "I'd be likin' that, I would."

He bent, his lips slowly brushing hers. Not questioning, or asking permission, but rather a slow, lazy exploration that promised it was only a beginning.

She sighed as his arms closed around her, drawing her into his embrace.

And then she was drifting…drifting…drifting… into a fine, white mist.

Chapter One

New Year's Eve: 1745
Inverness, Scotland

The dancing had stopped and people were now milling about, many of them walking away from the banks of the River Ness. Charlotte looked up at the attractive, dark-haired stranger she'd just finished kissing—the man knew how to kiss!—but instead of looking as bedazzled as she felt, he was only smiling politely.

Had her response not been enthusiastic enough? For a moment, she was tempted to wrap her arms around his neck and press herself against the length of him—it's what one of her daring heroines would have done—but he'd dropped her hand and stepped back. She didn't want to *leap* at him, so she just said, "I enjoyed that."

Let him think what he would.

"Aye. The dancin' gets a wee bit wild toward the end."

The dancing? What about the kiss?

He grinned, his smoky-gray eyes crinkling a bit. "'Tis *oidhche Challainn,* nae?"

Thankfully, she knew that was Gaelic for Hogmanay, since both Thea and Vi had cheat sheets with common Gaelic phrases. But what about the *kissing*? Did the man not remember it? Or was he so used to kissing women that it just wasn't that important? She gave a soft sigh. More than likely, with his skill, it was the latter. She forced a smile. It wouldn't do to let him think she was upset. She didn't even know the man.

"I suspect some people get a little bit too festive on Hogmanay."

"Aye, they do." He dipped his head slightly toward her. "Since no one is about to introduce us, I'm Niall Fraser."

"I'm Charlotte Campbell."

"Campbell?" The smile left his face. "What is a Campbell woman doing in Inverness?"

Charlotte frowned. "Why wouldn't I be?"

He didn't answer that but looked quickly around. "Do ye have kin with ye? How many? Where are they?"

She took a small step back, beginning to wonder if there was something wrong with him. Just like in Gothic novels when the super-sexy, hunky hero was a bit mad. It would be her luck.

"I…I'm with two friends. I probably should go find them."

She glanced toward the nearly empty street but didn't see either Thea or Vi. Of course, it was really dark… She blinked and squinted. The street lights had all gone out. A power outage maybe, since there were a few candles in windows. Other than that, the only light was the reflection of the moon off the water.

"I…don't see them," she said, "but I'm staying at the Best Western just across the river—"

"The what?" He lifted his head. "Where are ye staying?"

"There." She started to point then dropped her hand as her heart followed with a heavy thump to her stomach.

There was no hotel on the opposite bank.

"Where?" he asked again.

"I… I…" The world felt like it was suddenly spinning, and she stumbled slightly. Niall caught her arm and steadied her. "Tell me where your kin are, lass, and I'll escort ye to them."

"I don't know, exactly." She looked down the street. The cathedral didn't seem to be there either. She tried to think. Had someone laced a drink earlier? But she'd only had one glass of champagne before coming out into the street for the midnight festivities. Vi and Thea had shared the same bottle. She peered closer into the darkness. Where were they? Where were the familiar buildings? The cars? What was happening?

It felt surreal, much like a recurring dream she had of wanting to run but her legs wouldn't move. Slowly, she flexed a foot. It moved. At least, this wasn't a dream, then.

Had Brigadoon descended and swept her up? Was she experiencing something surreal? *Stop it!* Charlotte forced herself to rein in her imagination. She had *not* been transported to a mythical Scottish village that once, every hundred years, became visible to mortals who were allowed to enter its gates. She tried to shake her head to clear it, but it only made her feel lightheaded. She started to sway.

"I think I may be a bit tipsy…"

****

Niall looked down at the lass who'd just fainted in his arms. Part of her long, golden hair hid her face, the rest was draped over his arm and felt like silk. When he'd first seen her dancing in the circle, her hair flying out behind her, he'd been reminded of a faerie sylph floating through the air, her feet barely skimming the earth.

And she turned out to be a Campbell. Odd, though, that she should admit it, especially since Colonel John Campbell commanded the English forces here at Fort George. Did the lass not realize Bonnie Prince Charlie's followers were everywhere? Did she not ken this was enemy territory?

Perhaps she was daft. A pity for one so bonny, but she spoke with a strange accent. Her replies sounded confused and she wanted to go to some place called "best western." Best place in the western Highlands? Best place in the west Isles? He shook his head. She had pointed across the river to an empty space.

And where were her kin? If she were related to the colonel, soldiers would be everywhere. He looked around the deserted street again. He didn't see any, but other Campbells could be about. Just because he couldn't see them didn't mean they weren't out there. The Campbell tartan was dark like the Black Watch… He paused in his thinking and looked down at the woman he still held. Her tartan had lighter shades of green slashed through with orange stripes. Clan MacGregor. He frowned. They were rivals of the Campbells, but the MacGregors were also proscribed. Why on earth would she choose to wear the colors of a clan that had been publicly declared the enemy of the English government? Perhaps she figured Scots sympathetic to Prince Charlie would automatically accept a MacGregor as an ally. And most would. Perhaps she also knew she was in dangerous territory here in Inverness and thought the plaid would protect her. But then, why tell him her last name? None of it made sense.

Well. He was hardly solving the quandary by

standing like an eejit in the middle of an empty street past midnight. The woman had still not opened her eyes, although from her regular breathing she seemed to be sleeping.

"Lass?" He jostled her slightly. "Ye need to wake up."

"Hmmm," she murmured and buried her head against his shoulder much like a child who was worn out from play.

But she was no child. He was very much aware that one soft breast was also pressed against his chest and that her slumped body fitted quite nicely along the length of his.

He couldn't just leave her here. Niall looked around once more, but nothing moved in the shadows. Not that he was expecting movement. If her kin had been lurking about, they would have attacked him—or at least confronted him—by now. Charlotte Campbell was his responsibility, at least for the time being.

With a sigh, he stooped and slipped his free arm under her knees to lift her, which almost was his undoing since the skirt slipped and he could feel bare, smooth thighs. For a moment he wondered if the devil had been loosed this night and was beleaguering him with a beautiful, helpless woman in his arms.

He shifted his weight, adjusted his hold, and started walking. His own kin at Castle Dounie were used to him rescuing stray and hurt animals, but he'd never brought back a woman before.

Certainly not one who was a Campbell.

****

Charlotte awoke the next morning to bright sunshine and the wafting smell of cinnamon-scented oatmeal. For a moment she luxuriated in the soft downiness of the mattress and the warmth of a heavy wool blanket pulled up to her chin, allowing only her cheeks to feel the frigidness of the air.

Frigid air…had the thermostat in her room stopped working? Her eyes popped open and she stared at a pale blue canopy overhead. Where had that come from? Why was she in a four-poster bed? The blanket, she saw now, was a tartan of gray and blue squares with red-and-yellow lines. Where was she? Had a drink really been laced last night and she didn't make it back to the hotel?

"Well, then! I see ye are awake on this lovely morn!"

The voice didn't belong to anyone she recognized, and she slowly lifted her head to see a young woman in period Scottish dress beaming at her from across the room.

"Are ye hungry? I've brought porridge. Master Niall thought it would be just the thing to revive ye."

Niall. Events came flashing back. The man she had danced with. The man who didn't seem to remember kissing her.

"*Master* Niall?"

"Aye. The son of the laird."

"Son of a…" Charlotte stopped. She'd almost used a quite different word. An inappropriate word, but she wasn't thinking straight. "Why are you dressed like that?"

The girl glanced down and then gave her a confused look. ''Is something wrong with it?"

"Yes… No. *No.* I just wasn't…wasn't expecting anyone to still be in costume on New Year's Day."

The girl frowned. "'Tis me maid's dress."

"Maid? You're a maid?"

"Aye. Me name's Erin." She straightened her shoulders and smiled. "Shall I draw a bath for ye?"

"No. Not right now." A bath sounded heavenly, but Charlotte wasn't sure she wasn't hallucinating. Or maybe dreaming and conjuring up images to use in her next novel.

"Could you tell…Master…Niall that I'd like to speak to him?"

Erin's eyes rounded. "Ye want him to come to your bedchamber?"

"Um, no. Where could I meet with him?"

"This time of the mornin' he'll probably be breaking his fast in the Great Hall."

Charlotte closed her eyes briefly. Something was very much amiss here. Slowly, she pushed the covers aside and sat up, swinging her legs over the side of the tall bed. Her long skirt, bodice vest, and arisaidh were draped over the top of an armchair nearby, but she was still wearing the linen leine from last night, so she hadn't been completely undressed. Just *who* had undressed her? Her cheeks warmed as she wondered if it might have been Niall, and then she dismissed the thought. She still had on clothing, including underwear. And, she'd awakened alone.

"I suppose I need to get dressed, then."

"Ye'll probably nae want to be wearing that." Erin indicated her other clothing. "'Twould be too warm."

Warm? The room felt like a meat-locker in spite of the fire in the brazier near the small table where the rapidly cooling porridge sat. That heavy shawl would feel good right now, but she didn't really want to leave the room wearing an eighteenth-century costume. 'Is there something you could lend me?"

"Och, aye. I think ye are about the same size as Greer."

"Greer?"

"Master Niall's sister."

Had she met his sister? She didn't even remember getting here. Wherever *here* was. Confusion and questions were piling on top of each other, but if she wanted answers, she'd have to get dressed.

"Yes. Please. Tell her I'll be obliged."

Erin nodded and left, returning in a few moments carrying what looked like a mound of clothing. She spread it out on the bed. "She said ye can choose."

Charlotte looked over the array and tried to squelch a growing uneasiness. All of the dresses—gowns, really—were long, with voluptuous full skirts, nipped in waists, low necklines, and fitted sleeves. Costume period pieces. Or…were they? She tamped down the wave of hysteria that had begun to rise. Maybe Brigadoon had descended after all.

Where in the world was she? Charlotte glanced at Erin and decided it was probably not her best idea to ask what would sound like an idiotic question. She picked up a soft bluish-green wool.

"I'll try this one."

"'Tis a good choice. It will go with your eyes."

She hadn't thought about how she would look, but perhaps she should be more mindful. Men—at least in her novels—responded better to ladies who looked well-put-together. And she desperately needed some answers.

Ten minutes later, she was ready. Her tummy had been fortified with porridge and Erin had managed to pile her hair on top of her head in an arrangement of curls and had even pinched her cheeks to make them pinker. She almost laughed at that since the heroines in her stories did the same, but she suspected Erin wasn't aiding a flirtation since, when Charlotte caught a look at herself in the small mirror on the dresser, she'd looked as pale as a ghostly wraith.

She took a deep breath—thankfully, there had been no corset involved in dressing—and opened the door to step into the hall.

This was it, then. A moment of truth.

****

Niall tried to ignore the covert glances of his family seated around a small table near the dais in the Great Hall. They rarely used the actual formal table to break their fast, but this morning he wished they had, for it would have eliminated them all trying not to stare at him.

He swallowed the porridge which, while usually smooth and creamy, left a lump in his throat. He took a bit of barley bread, usually equally moist but today felt like dry hay in his mouth. He reached for the watered-down ale and then put it down and looked up.

His father studied him thoughtfully, his face passive and not giving any clue to what he was feeling, but he never revealed his feelings. The old man was wily as a fox, which was partly the reason he'd earned the moniker of "The Fox."

His sister's face was full of concern, although whether because he was not wolfing down his food like he usually did or because of his latest rescue, he wasn't sure. His brother, Simon, had devilment in his eyes. He was probably only holding back some raucous remark about Charlotte because their sister Greer had just joined them.

Niall shifted in his chair. “I doona have any more answers for ye than I did last night.”

“Ye ken nothing about her?” Simon grinned, the slightest hint of innuendo in his voice. “She’s quite bonny.”

Their father shifted his gaze to his oldest son. “At the moment we are nae concerned with her looks.”

Simon sobered and his father looked back at Niall. “She told ye she had nae kin?”

“She said she had two friends, but I wasna able to find them.”

They’d had this conversation last night after he’d brought Charlotte, still unconscious, home. His father liked to re-word his inquiries as a way to check if the person he was questioning was consistent or lying, a trait he was well-versed in. His father also had an instinct for discerning when someone was withholding information, which was probably why his father was studying him so carefully this morning.

He hadn’t told them Charlotte’s last name. He wasn’t exactly sure why he was protecting her. If more Campbells—besides the colonel—were in the vicinity, they could pose a real danger. His father, as laird, certainly should be made aware. For that matter, a message should also be sent to Charles Stuart’s camp, alerting them.

Yet he held back. He had not seen any Campbell tartans last night, although it would be easy enough to disguise themselves. The fact that no one had come to claim Charlotte had been more telling, especially when the crowds were gone and he was carrying her to his horse. He’d stationed several of his men along the route home to Castle Dounie just to make sure they weren’t being followed. All of the men had reported the road had been clear.

"I will try to find out more when I talk to her this morning."

"If she's awake." His brother shrugged. "I suppose 'tis possible she had a head injury before she fell against ye."

He hadn't thought of that. Sometimes it took a little while before the effects took place. It might also explain her confusing answers. "Mayhap we should sent for the physician if she still sleeps."

"She's awake," Greer said. "And apparently not worse for wear. Erin came to my room to borrow a gown or two."

Niall breathed a sigh of relief. "'Tis good news, then."

"Aye." His father fixed him with a stern look. "We need to ken who the lass is and why she is wandering about without kin. I expect ye to get the answers."

"I intend to," Niall answered.

He knew his father's look. If he didn't get a satisfactory explanation from Charlotte, his father would.

****

Niall was no longer in the Great Hall when she went down, but she found him in a room across the way. For a moment she stood in the doorway silently, taking in the scene.

A large mahogany desk took up most of the center of the room, a huge, throne-like leather chair behind it. Two smaller, straight-back wooden chairs were directly in front, which reminded her of the principal's office at her high school. As a rather independent-thinking teenager, she'd been summoned to his presence on more than one occasion.

She felt like that now, except this room didn't look at all modern. An oil painting between two wooden bookcases on the wall behind the desk depicted a hunting scene with men in seventeenth-century dress, and the tapestry hung on the stone wall by the narrow window was positively medieval-looking. A substantial fire blazed from the open hearth opposite the desk, casting dancing shadows across the floor and over two comfortable-looking armchairs. The only other light source were two oil lamps in sconces and a candle burning on the desk a safe distance from the ledger that Niall was working on.

Uneasiness stirred in her stomach again. She obviously was in some sort of actual castle probably a couple of centuries old, but did they have to keep everything so authentic?

She cleared her throat and he looked up. For a moment he studied her, then he smiled, marked his spot in the ledger with a piece of paper, and shut it, then gestured her to enter.

"Please. Have a seat."

Since he was sitting behind the desk, she sat down in one of straight-backs. At least Niall didn't look like the old, bespectacled principal who never changed his expression.

"How are ye feeling this morning?" Niall asked.

"Better." She didn't really know if she was better or not since she must have had some kind of blackout. "I know this sounds silly, but where am I, exactly?"

He only inclined his head. "Ye are at Castle Dounie, near Beauly."

Beauly. Vaguely, she recalled it was a village near Inverness. “How…How did I get here?”

He didn’t seem to think that an odd question either. “I brought ye here on my horse after ye swooned.”

Her fictional heroines *swooned.* She had never fainted in her life. But there really wasn’t much point in saying that since she didn’t know exactly what had happened.

Something had happened. “I’m afraid I don’t recall.”

This time he frowned. “Could ye have fallen and hit your head sometime yesterday?”

“No. I was perfectly fine.” That popped out before she had time to think on it. Maybe she should have said yes and claimed a concussion to give herself time to sort things out. Well, too late now. “Umm. I might have had a bit too much of your whisky. It’s very strong. Could you…could you enlighten me on what happened?”

“I saw ye at the revelry last eve. I joined ye in the dance.” He looked at her closely. “Do ye remember that?” When she nodded, he went on. “We introduced ourselves. And then, ye just swooned. I caught ye before ye could fall.”

“You didn’t kiss me?”

“Kiss ye?” He blinked. Then he grinned, the dimple showing in his cheek. “I think I would have remembered that, lass.”

So Niall didn’t kiss her? Had she dreamed it? She felt her face warm as he was now gazing at her with a look of intense interest. Better to change the subject. She looked around.

“This is your home?”

“Aye. ’Tis the seat of Clan Fraser of Lovat. My father’s the laird.”

Laird. She supposed maybe the Scottish equivalent to English aristocracy might still use the term. If she recalled, Frasers were the dominant clan in this area. "I think it's wonderful that the clans still take so much pride in their ancestry."

"Still?"

"Well…yes. I mean, Scotland is part of the United Kingdom—"

"United kingdom?" He snorted. "We may be under George's sovereign rule at present, but that's about to change."

"George? Don't you mean King Charles?"

"Well, aye. Good of ye to call him that, although he has nae been crowned yet." Niall shrugged. "'Tis just a matter of time, though, before a Stuart king is on the throne again."

A *Stuart* king. Not Queen Elizabeth's son, but Bonnie Prince Charlie—who would also have been Charles III. It couldn't be. And then, as if to reinforce the impossible thought, she saw the date on the paper he'd used as a bookmark.

January 1, 1746.

1746. The year the battle of Culloden was fought. The year the Jacobites lost everything to the English. Her head began to spin again and she clutched the desk rim for balance as she started to sway.

Niall leapt up from behind the desk and was beside her, steadying her. She took a deep breath. At least, he was *real*. She wasn't imagining his strong, warm hands on her arms or the way he was gently rubbing them. He was *real*. The year could not be 1746. It wasn't possible to time-travel.

Was it?

Chapter Two

"What did ye discover?"

Niall turned away from the window where he'd been looking over the empty, snow-patched hills and looked at his brother.

"Nothing in particular."

Simon's eyebrows rose. "Nothing?"

"Nothing of value." He took his seat behind the desk again. "The lass was still nae feeling well. I didna want to press her too much."

Simon grinned as he turned a chair around and straddled it. "I would think ye might want to *press* her quite close."

Niall gave him an irritated look. "Charlotte is a guest here. We doona take advantage."

"Charlotte, is it? 'Tis a bit familiar, is it nae?" His brother continued to grin. "For someone who doesna want to take advantage, I mean."

"Will ye stop!"

The smile wavered and stopped. "What is it ye are nae telling us?"

Niall clenched his fists beneath the desk. His brother had the same uncanny sense of sniffing out what was hidden behind words as his father did. He couldn't—wouldn't—share any information until he could find out why Charlotte had been wearing a MacGregor tartan when she told him her last name was Campbell. Had she been trying to disguise herself and inadvertently blurted out her name without thinking? Whisky had flowed freely last night, and she had said something about imbibing. While he doubted his father would do anything so drastic as to lock her away as a prisoner, things were too volatile to be sure what he *would* do.

And in too much turmoil. Prince Charlie's army had successfully reached Edinburgh before Christmas, but the castle had been retaken when he marched south to gather more troops. The siege on Carlisle had worked, but the prince was still waiting on French troops to arrive to aid the clans. Some of the clans, like the MacIntosh, were evenly divided in their loyalty. Word that there might be a Campbell spy near Inverness would not set well. He sighed.

"I call her Charlotte because that is the name she gave me leave to." She hadn't precisely given him permission to use her Christian name, but she offered it instead of referring to herself as "Miss." Besides, this wasn't England and their etiquette didn't really apply in the Highlands. "I intend to question her further, but as I said, she was nae feeling well and returned to her room."

Simon gave him an appraising look before he rose from the chair. "Doona wait too long, brother. A woman who appears out of nowhere with no kin to chaperone or claim her is nae one to be trusted."

"I ken that." So far, only his family and Erin knew the circumstances about Charlotte's arrival. Once more of the servants saw her, rumors would start as well. "I'll have answers for ye before sundown. I vow it."

Simon nodded and moved to the door. As he left, Niall leaned back in his chair. There was definitely one question he wanted an answer to, but it wasn't one he could probably ask.

Charlotte had mentioned that he'd kissed her. She hadn't said she'd *wished* he'd kissed her. She hadn't flirtatiously implied she wanted him to now. She had sounded completely sincere that he *had* kissed her last night and looked a little hurt by his reply. His reply had been truthful. He *would* have remembered kissing her, especially since he would have liked nothing better than to kiss her again. But it hadn't happened.

Uneasily, he wondered if Charlotte might be somewhat barmy. Perhaps she had escaped from an asylum where her family had confined her and she only *thought* she was a Campbell.

The thought was strangely unsettling.

****

Charlotte knew she couldn't hide in her room for much longer. Erin had already brought up a tray for the noonday meal since she'd pleaded a headache, which wasn't entirely false.

Her mind was spinning, trying to make sense of what was happening or, more precisely, *when* it was happening. She was in Scotland. In 1746. Impossible. But…in the twenty-first century, Castle Dounie was only a ruin. Beaufort Castle had replaced it. So. How could it be she was here?

She was still pondering that thought as she made her way back to the library-study later that afternoon. This time she had been summoned. Actually, the note Erin had delivered from Niall a short time ago had "requested" her presence, but she figured that was rather like a teacher "requesting" a student to "please have a seat." The teacher meant *Sit down. Now*. Niall had meant *Come down. Now.*

This time he was waiting for her as she entered the library. The ledger with its telltale date was nowhere in sight. Instead, a small teapot with two pewter mugs and a plate of shortbread were on the desktop. Perhaps he—or maybe Greer—had decided a more social setting would be better for the interrogation. For interrogation it would be. She had no doubt about that. She took a deep breath. At least, her interrogator was easy to gaze upon. Very much so.

Sunshine was streaming through the window, casting a bluish tone to his pitch hair, which was long enough to curl off the collar of the shirt he wore. The light accentuated the angle of his face: high cheekbones, squared jaw, straight nose. It was his eyes, though, that were really fascinating. Neither brown nor gray, they were more the color of dark smoke. Right now, they were trained on her. She sat.

"Tea?" he asked, lifting the pot.

"Please." Charlotte fought a hysterical laugh that threatened to escape. How ironical to be having tea as though this were a social visit.

He poured, then smiled as he moved the cup toward her. "I'll let ye put in the sugar and cream. I'm nae good at this kind of thing."

It was a disarming statement, as was the smile, but it did nothing to relax her. Quite the opposite. She was pretty sure she'd choke on the tea if she tried to swallow. Still, she added a dollop of cream and pretended to take a sip, thankful her hand was steady enough not to spill the stuff. She set the cup down.

"I suppose you have questions?"

An eyebrow lifted. "Aye. I'll let ye start, though. Tell me how ye came to be at the dance last night."

So there *had* been a dance. At least she hadn't imagined that. Just the kiss. Her eyes drifted to his mouth. It was a very kissable mouth, wide and full. Maybe she had just wanted to kiss him?

The hysterical bubble threatened to rise again.

"Yes. Well." She forced herself to focus on the desk in front of her. She had a half-baked story that she thought might be believed since she could hardly tell him she was from the future. She'd be locked away for sure.

"I was at the dance with two of my friends. Vi Sutherland and Thea Ross. I…think they might have met some gentlemen…" She gave him what she hoped was a conspiratorial smile. "If you know what I mean. They're probably looking for me—"

"Sutherland? Ross?" he interrupted. "Who accompanied them?"

She frowned. He'd certainly missed her point. "No one."

He frowned too. "Lass. Ye need to tell me the truth."

"I…am." So far, she was. "We just wanted to mingle with the townspeople."

Niall leaned forward, his elbows on the desk. "Ye are expecting me to believe that three women—all of whose clans back the government and would like nothing better than to capture Prince Charlie—just happened to be in Inverness by yourselves?"

Instinctively, Charlotte leaned back as comprehension dawned. Their ancestors had been anti-Jacobites. The Campbells had fought for the English at Culloden, as had the clans of Ross and Sutherland. *Good Lord.* Did Niall think they—*she*—was a spy?

"I… We…" She swallowed. "Actually, we didn't want our families to know we were gone."

His eyes narrowed slightly. 'I doona believe ye, lass."

"You…don't?" She swallowed again. "Why not?"

He held up his hand and ticked off reasons. "One. Your *friends* never showed up last night. Two. Ye are a fair distance from Argyll. How did ye make that trip by yourself? Three—"

"I didn't make the trip by myself. I was with my friends."

"Three," he continued counting on his fingers. "Ye wore a MacGregor tartan instead of a Campbell one, to disguise who you were."

"Disguise? No." Good grief. She'd rented the costume and hadn't bothered to ask about which clan it represented.

"Ye expect me to believe Campbells are nae hiding down the road waiting for ye to return to camp?"

"No. Yes. I mean… I do not know if there are Campbells lurking somewhere. I would hope not."

"Ye hope not? Why would ye nae want your kin near?"

"I…" What kind of an explanation could she come up with? Her imagination began to stir. What would the plot be if she were writing this? She was in enemy territory, in disguise, a fair distance from the clan seat… Inspiration hit in the form of a well-used—maybe *over*-used—romance trope. But. This was the eighteenth century, not the twenty-first. Jane Austin and the Bronte sisters hadn't been born yet. It might work. She took a deep breath and had the ironic thought that his handsome face would serve well as that of her hero, although at this point that was stretching even her imagination too far. All she could do was hope he'd believe her story.

"All right. I haven't been *totally* truthful." She ventured a tentative smile but he remained impassive. "I was afraid you'd send me back."

Still no smile. "Send ye back?"

"Yes. To…" What was the name of the Campbell seat? She nearly panicked as she drew a blank and then remembered. "Inveraray—"

"Ye are kin to Archibald Campbell?"

"Ah…indirectly." She supposed that was true, if she traced her genealogy back far enough. "In any event," Charlotte went on before Niall could question her further, "my father betrothed me to a man I do not want to marry, and the laird approved it. So…" She shrugged. "I disguised myself and ran away." Now the lie was out, she felt strangely calm. "My friends helped me escape."

Niall leaned back and considered. "And where were ye planning to go?"

"I…hadn't quite thought that far." That much was true. She was making this up as she went along. "I…just needed to get away."

Her *plot* now needed an ending. She'd never been an author who flew by the seat of her pants. "Will you help me?"

Niall studied her for so long she was beginning to think he wasn't going to. Or, maybe, he was going to turn her out on her ear. Or call a magistrate…

"For now," he said.

"What?" She wanted to make sure she had heard correctly.

A corner of his mouth lifted in a half-smile. "I said 'for now.' I will help ye for now. But…" The smile faded. "Ye had best nae be lying to me."

****

"So ye believe the lass, then?" his father asked.

They were sitting in the small room—the council room, adjacent to the Great Hall—usually used for arranging truces with rival clans. Although it was only his family that was gathered—father, brother, sister—Niall felt the weight of his conclusion as strongly as if he'd been negotiating with King George himself. The safety of his clan was at stake.

"I want to give the lass shelter."

Simon grinned. "Of course ye do."

Niall slanted him a look. "'Tis the Highland way to offer hospitality."

This time his brother snorted. "Ye might try and convince the Donalds of Glen Coe of that. Too bad none of them are left because the Campbells finished them off."

Niall had told his family what had transpired earlier during his conversation with Charlotte, including her last name. "Ye canna blame the lass for something that happened fifty years ago."

"And it wasna Clan Campbell that attacked the Donalds," Greer said. "'Twas one commander acting on orders from King William. Besides," she added, "I doona think Charlotte is going to massacre anybody."

"Ye miss the point, sister." Simon replied. "'Tis her kin that may be lurking about. Or, she might be a scout for Colonel Campbell."

"'Tis true the Campbells are nae to be trusted, especially in these times," their father said, "but I have sent out men to scour the area. Each party has one messenger on a fast horse to report back if they find anything suspicious. So far, nothing. No soldiers waiting, either."

"'Tis only been an hour, Da," Simon said.

His brother was right. An hour wasn't long to search, especially if the Campbell men weren't soldiers or wearing their plaids. And, while men from Argyll may not be familiar with the mountainous terrain around Inverness, they would know how to hide since their own territory near the Trossachs included wooded glens, braes, and lochs that were generally mist-covered and ideal for disappearing into. The MacGregors had been doing it for centuries.

Which brought Niall's thoughts back to Charlotte's disguise. It had either been complete foolishness on her part to risk wearing that tartan or sheer genius.

"Ye look troubled," Greer said.

He forced a smile, although he knew his sister was astute enough not be fooled by it. "I was just thinking it might be wise if we didna mention her last name to the rest of our people."

His father frowned. "I doona like to be deceitful."

Niall refrained from snorting. His father was a master at being deceitful. It was something Niall had trouble rationalizing, but he'd been witness to it on more occasions that he wanted to think about.

"Niall has a point," Greer said. "We canna guarantee that someone would nae want to seek revenge because of the name."

"Ye think someone would openly defy me?"

"'Tis troubling times," Simon said. "Nae all the men who pledge allegiance to the Cause have pledged fealty to ye, Da."

Their father's face grew stormy for an instant, then smoothed to its usual passiveness. "Ye think nae?"

"If there are some," Niall said quickly, "why stir up

a hornet's nest that might lead to suspicion? The lass arrived in MacGregor colors. 'Tis easier to let people think 'tis her clan. We know the difference and we can keep a watchful eye."

Simon considered, then turned to his father. "Do ye nae agree? 'Twould avoid a problem."

The old man grimaced. "I will concede the point. I would rather concentrate on preparing the men to fight for Prince Charlie."

"That's settled, then," Niall said with relief as they all stood to go out to dinner. He was nearly at the door behind his father and sister when Simon put a restraining hand on his arm.

"'Tis something nae right about this, brother." He released his hold. "Ye had best take care that the lass is who she says she is."

Chapter Three

Charlotte stood on the bank of the River Ness once more and looked around. Last night at dinner Niall had suggested that they go into Inverness this morning to see if she could locate her two friends.

Dinner. It had gone better than Charlotte had expected. They'd eaten in the Great Hall, which had been filled with hundreds of Frasers, but Niall's family hadn't sat at the raised dais. Instead, they had a smaller round table off to one side where, as Greer pointed out, they could observe their kinsmen without being on display themselves.

It had helped to keep Charlotte's presence obscure as well. Heads had turned when she'd walked in with the laird, but he'd introduced her as a friend of distant MacGregor kin who would be staying with them for a while. That his clan had accepted that simple statement and returned to their own conversations spoke volumes as to what kind of authority a laird had in the eighteenth century.

Authority that could land her in dire straits if he found out the truth.

But this morning she had her mind on other matters. Both Niall's brother and sister had accompanied them, which meant she was going to have to convince three people of whatever story she could concoct. Not too much different than creating sub-plots, she tried to tell herself. She was a writer, after all.

She looked down the street to where a horse and carriage waited outside what appeared to be a general store. Several riders passed them, one or two tipping a hat toward their little group. Other than that, there wasn't much going on.

Were Vi and Thea here? Had they somehow travelled with her through Time? She doubted it, since they hadn't been together when whatever it was had happened to transport her. Vi had still been standing on the bank, and Thea had gone to check on the fallen man. Only she had joined the circle of dancing. And Niall had been there…but had that been in the twenty-first century or this one?

"Where did ye say ye were staying?" Greer asked, breaking through her thoughts. "We can check to see if your friends have returned."

She had been staying at the Best Western. Which hadn't yet been built. She looked across the river. Only a few small buildings lined the other side, none of which looked like an inn. Not that she'd be registered at one anyway.

"We…hadn't actually checked in anywhere."

While Greer widened her eyes in surprise, Simon narrowed his. "Doona tell me that three women thought to camp outside."

"Well, no." The words were out before she could give them much thought. So exactly where would three women—alone—stay? *Think.* Inspiration hit. New Year's Eve celebrations drew crowds, regardless of the century.

"The places we tried were all full." Three pairs of eyes watched her, waiting for her to continue.

"We…thought…if we joined the dancing, maybe we could ask someone for accommodation afterward." That sounded plausible. She hoped. "That must have been what happened to my friends. They found someone hospitable enough to offer them shelter."

She sensed Niall was studying her. Her previous version had intimated that her friends had disappeared to couple. Were the two ideas so far apart? Thankfully, he didn't question her.

"Well, if we were in Beauly, we could solve that mystery quickly since there are nae that many homes," Greer said, "but Inverness has nearly ten thousand people, not to mention other visitors."

Thank goodness for that. "I'm not sure what we can do."

"Your friends will probably start checking the inns," Greer said. "Mayhap they've already checked some of them. At the least, we could ask the innkeepers to put up signs indicating that you're staying at Castle Dounie "

"We decided it was safer nae to call Charlotte a Campbell," Niall turned to her. "Would your friends make a connection to MacGregor?"

"They…might. Thea chose the MacGregor tartan for me." That much was true, albeit it she had picked it out from a costume shop in Edinburgh. Still, both Vi and Thea were more expert about actual Scottish history than she was. They might—if they were in this century—make the connection. "I think it's worth a try."

Greer smiled and Niall nodded. "We'll do it, then."

Only Simon looked skeptical. Charlotte wasn't sure if that was because he didn't think the idea wouldn't work or because he didn't believe *her*.

****

When they returned to the castle, there was palatable excitement in the air. Niall could feel it even before one of men came rushing toward him and Simon. “Good news, my lords, good news!”

Another man approached. “Your father is waiting for the both of ye.”

His father was actually grinning when they joined him in the council room off the Great Hall. His father had seldom even broken a smile these past months while Prince Charlie had gone south to recruit more troops and not been overly successful, having crossed back into Scotland just before Christmas. Niall wondered if he was contemplating which side to back. He’d done it before in the first Uprising, or so Niall had been told. He’d been a wee bairn. He hoped his father was serious about backing Prince Charlie. “Do ye have good news about the Campbells or the prince?” he asked as he sat down.

“Both,” his father answered. “My men didna find any Campbells lurking about nor did anyone else they questioned, so your lass may be telling the truth.”

Your lass. *His* lass. Of course, Charlotte wasn’t his. She was a stranger who had fallen into his arms. Literally. Still. He couldn’t deny that he rather liked the sound of the phrase. Liked the idea, too. She was bonny, as his brother had pointed out, but there was an inner strength to her. She’d had the courage to run away from a situation she didn’t want. He sensed there was more to the situation than what she’d told him, but he’d give her time for the telling of it. And, he realized, he wanted to spend more time with her. Wanted to hold her—this time while she was conscious—and kiss her…

“Are ye back with the living?”

Niall blinked at Simon’s words and then felt an

unfamiliar heat crawl up his neck. *Contrachd*! Curses! Had he actually been traipsing away in fantasy like a complete eejit while his father had important news?

"I was just thinking we can put more trust in the lass now."

"Aye. Trust." Simon didn't look fooled for a moment. "If that is what ye want to call it."

He refused to take the bait and turned to his father. "Do ye have news on Prince Charlie as well?"

"Aye. Ye ken Glasgow was nae particularly welcoming when he returned, in spite of the balls he hosted, but," his father's grin widened, "he managed to nae only secure several thousand pounds, but the Provost agreed to outfit all six thousand troops with new uniforms and boots."

That, in itself, was worth a small fortune. With the worst of the winter onset in the next few weeks, it was also much needed, for survival as well as morale. But another thought struck him.

"Six thousand men? Prince Charlie is near his goal, then."

"Aye. 'Tis another bit of good news as well. Cumberland is still in London, which leaves General Hawley in charge of the government troops in Scotland."

That was good news, or at least as good as it could get if there were going to be *any* government troops in Scotland. The duke was the third son of the king and had gotten a formidable reputation for brutal violence on the Continent during the conflict over the Austrian succession. Having him out of the country—even temporarily—was good. King George must have heard rumors that the French were planning to aid Prince Charlie and wanted Cumberland on the home front since

France's easiest entry ports would be along the eastern coast of England.

"So what is next?" Simon asked.

"I've sent word to my brother Charles at Inverallochy to prepare our men in case the prince issues a call-to-arms," his father said. "I'm a wee bit too long in the tooth to lead the men myself."

His father certainly looked braw enough, even though the man was in his seventies. And cagey. Niall raised his brows. "Do ye think my uncle will try to engage Hawley?"

"Mayhap. I think Prince Charlie has his eye on Stirling Castle, though," his father answered. "'Twould be an opportune time to attack."

"The castle is well-fortified," Niall said, "even if the garrison itself numbers only a few hundred men."

"Aye. Well, the word is the townspeople will nae hold out long," his father answered, "so a siege may be just as beneficial. Prince Charlie's troops will have food and shelter. They can starve out the garrison."

Simon leaned back and smiled. "Sounds like we may be on our way to independence."

Niall nodded his acquiescence, although something niggled at him, like there were too many questions left unanswered. He just wasn't sure whether it was about Scotland's future or the future of the lass he'd brought home.

****

Thankfully, everyone was abuzz about the news that had been delivered and Charlotte wasn't asked many questions at dinner that night. Even better, no one was staring at her with *unanswered* questions in their eyes.

Because she didn't have the answers.

"Ye look tired," Greer said as she held out a plate of bannocks.

Charlotte took one. The scone-like bread was baked with oatmeal and had a wonderful heartiness to it, especially when she added fresh-churned butter from the creamery shed. Just what she needed.

"I guess I am. Visiting the inns today was stressful."

"Aye. I can imagine. 'Tis never easy when a friend or kin goes missing." Greer set the plate down. "But doona give up hope that we'll find them."

Charlotte didn't want to squelch any hope, but she suspected Thea and Vi were still in the twenty-first century. Or, rather, *would be* in the twenty-first century. It was really hard to wrap her head around the fact that she'd actually time-traveled.

She still didn't know how, either. While they had been in Inverness earlier, she'd made a point of standing on the bank where she had stood with her friends. She'd retraced her steps toward where the dance had taken place on the riverbank, ostensibly to enjoy the view. She'd even walked widdershins in an oblong circle, since that was the direction she'd been dancing in—from what she recalled—when she felt herself drifting. She'd felt pretty stupid doing that, since she vaguely recalled moving counter-clockwise as the direction witches danced in. Not that she thought witchcraft had anything to do with what happened, but she had wondered about magic.

Nothing had happened. Except for the absence of the Best Western and the cathedral, the landscape looked remarkably like it had in the twenty-first century.

"I guess we'll just have to wait and see if my friends turn up," she said. "I don't know what else we can do."

"Well, at least there is nae fighting in the area right now nor anyone lurking about that might think to abduct them."

Charlotte frowned. "How do you know that?"

Greer paused, her face turning pink. "Da had men out last night searching."

"For my friends?" The words were no sooner out of her mouth than she knew what Greer meant. Her father had men out searching for Campbells. Spies.

Her story had not been completely accepted, then. She shouldn't be surprised, since their father was laird and had a responsibility to his clan. She suspected Simon doubted her as well. Every time she caught him looking at her, it was with skepticism on his face. She wondered if Niall believed her. She needed him to, even though her tale wasn't true. She suspected he'd probably hate her if he found out she was lying. In the short amount of time she'd been with him, she knew he was honorable and honest. Traits she cherished. Traits she wished she could share. Who would believe her if she told the truth? She couldn't risk it, because being put in an asylum in the eighteenth century meant to be forgotten and left to perish.

Still, she *was* in the eighteenth century. There must be some reason she'd been transported here.

The buzz of the conversation around her became louder and she became aware of how, suddenly, everyone was voicing confidence that it wouldn't take long to defeat King George now. The Scots' numbers were growing and they'd had success at Prestopans and Carlisle. Soon, Scotland would be independent again.

But it wouldn't. The battle at Culloden loomed ahead. Not only would Scotland be defeated, there would be hundreds—thousands—of lives lost in the battle. The Frasers had been at the front lines. She looked across the table at Niall. Would he be one of them?

Sorrow and a sense of hopelessness shot through her, and it wasn't for her friends Thea and Vi. It was because Niall might be killed in that battle.

Could she prevent it? Was that why she'd landed in this century somehow? To prevent the battle at Culloden from happening?

Chapter Four

Now that Charlotte had a goal—or at least, a *possible* reason why she might have been transported through Time—she had planning to do.

Her mind had started spinning at dinner, much like it did when inspiration hit for a new novel, except this wasn't a fictional story. This was real. With real consequences.

She pulled the soft woolen robe more closely around herself as she settled in the armchair near the brazier in her room, letting the heat warm her toes. She was going to have to be careful going about this, since women's opinions in the eighteenth century weren't necessarily valued. For that matter, she wasn't sure how much they were valued in the twenty-first century either, given the global state of affairs. But no matter. In either century, it wouldn't do to claim to know the future.

Especially a future that spelled the defeat of Scotland.

Her grasp of historical details was only fair, since she concentrated on dashing, kilted heroes more than their political times. Too bad she didn't have her cell phone so she could Google what she needed to know. Not that there were any cell towers around. A somewhat hysterical giggle bubbled in her throat. What would Niall think if he saw her talking into a piece of plastic? Or—the giggle broke free—having that thing *answer* her.

Just as well, then, that her phone was lying in a Best Western hotel room 200-plus years in the future.

The giggle subsided. She needed to concentrate.

Fifteen hundred Scots had lost their lives at Culloden. She knew Clan Fraser had been one of the largest regiments in the battle, but that was probably to be expected since this area was their ancestral seat. Had—would—Niall be one of them? She closed her eyes and rubbed her temples. *No*. Not if she could help it.

She opened her eyes and stared into the glow of the small fire by her feet. The flames sputtered, changing color from red to blue, a few of them reaching higher before subsiding. The writer in her couldn't help the analogy of the English Redcoats and the Scottish blue flag, the rising and fall of the flames indicative of which battles each side had won. So far.

She sighed and rose, walking to the window to gaze out at the night. There was so much she needed to know. Who were the real men in charge? What kind of strategy were they planning to use? What were the actual plans? She couldn't thwart anything if she only conjectured.

But what sources did she have? Niall's father would certainly have historical background, given his age, but she recalled suddenly—why hadn't she connected it before?—that the man had a shady past. She'd done research for a series on bustlers and hustlers of the past and the 11th Lord Lovat's name had come up. He'd told the Jacobites—the first time around with the Old Pretender—that he sided with them, but had written a letter to Queen Anne saying he was pro-government. If she remembered correctly, he'd been outed and fled to France for awhile. One Internet article had called him the "most notorious double-agent of his time." Probably not a good source to trust with questions.

Niall's brother Simon was already suspicious of her. Not a good source for answers either. Greer wouldn't be privy to war strategies or plans either because she was female. That left Niall.

She would have to be very, very careful in how she extracted information from him. She couldn't afford to alienate him. Nor did she want to. She needed to earn his trust if she were going to have any chance of him believing her when the time came.

She had the queasy feeling that the ground was moving beneath her, much like the dangerous bogs surrounding Drummossie Moor where Culloden had been fought.

****

Shopping in the eighteenth century wasn't so entirely different than in the twenty-first. That is, if one counted mortar-and-brick stores only, since there were no on-line options.

"I like that gown!" Greer pointed to a ready-made hanging in a shop window on one of Inverness' side streets. "The color would be perfect for you. Let's see if it fits." Without waiting for an answer she flung the door open and went inside.

Charlotte exchanged glances with Niall, who had accompanied them. He wore the same stoic expression she'd seen on men sitting in the center of malls waiting for their wives to come back from wherever they were using their credit cards. She gave him a tentative smile as they followed Greer.

"We shouldn't be long. Just one or two things."

"Hmph. Ye doona ken my sister."

She supposed he might have a point. Greer was

something of a whirlwind, full of energy and not reticent at all. She offered her opinion freely and didn't seem to notice Simon—or even their father—frowning at her. Or, more likely, she didn't care. Vi would have liked her. A 1700s version of a women's libber.

She had also arranged this shopping trip. When Charlotte had mentioned she couldn't pay for anything—her "friends" must have picked up her bag along with theirs—Greer had given her a practical look. *I doona mind sharing my clothes with ye, but ye should have some of your own.* Then she'd smiled conspiratorially. *Besides, if I divide my clothing with ye, I will just have to make up for it.*

So, here they were. The dress—a soft woolen that felt like cashmere—fit.

"Excellent!" Greer exclaimed and turned to the proprietor. "We'll take three more in different colors."

The man nodded. "I'll have to order the material, but—"

"That's too much trouble," Charlotte said. "This one will be fine."

"Nonsense." Greer shook her head. "Ye cannae have just one." She turned back to the shop owner. "Order enough material for four."

Charlotte widened her eyes. "But—"

"Nae another word," Greer said and moved to a table that had an assortment of scarves, stockings, and other accessories. She gathered up an armful and took them to the counter. "We'll need some linen shifts, too."

"Right over there." He pointed.

Greer added several of those to her stack as well. "Ye can send the bill to my da at Castle Dounie."

"Castle Dounie? Of course." The man wrapped the

purchases and handed them to Niall, who took them with a resigned look.

Once they were out on the street, Charlotte turned to Greer and Niall. "I cannot thank you enough for your generosity."

"Oh, we are nae done yet," Greer answered cheerfully. " There are boots to buy, and slippers. And ye'll need at least one bonnet."

"No, really—"

"And a cloak as well," Greer said. "Come on, then. I ken just the place." She was off, leaving Charlotte and Niall to trail in her wake.

Charlotte slanted a look at Niall, expecting to see him scowling, but his face was impassive, so perhaps he was used to his sister's tenaciousness. He had warned her earlier. He smiled slightly.

"She's getting away from us, lass."

Charlotte smiled back, appreciating his humor. Most of the men she knew wouldn't have been so patient.

Still, a small sigh escaped him as they followed his sister's trail.

****

Niall wasn't quite sure if he considered himself Scotland's biggest eejit or a valiant bodyguard. In either case, here he was escorting Charlotte and his sister while they shopped for gowns and slippers, bonnets, and other female paraphernalia.

He should be back at the castle conferring with his brother regarding the advance on Stirling. Instead, he was loaded down with an assortment of bags and boxes that contained purchases.

Maybe no one would spot him.

He should have known it would be bad luck to even

think that thought. No sooner had he done so when he heard a hearty voice hale him. Slowly he turned—his vision was half-obscured—to see his friend Keir Gordon crossing the street. Keir's sister, Fiona, was with him.

Double trouble.

"*Madainn mhath*," he said.

"Mornin' to ye too," Keir answered, his lips quirking as he eyed the various packages Niall was toting. Then his gaze turned to Charlotte and his grin widened.

"Well, now, who be ye?"

"I'm Charlotte—"

"MacGregor," Niall said before she could finish. "She's visiting us."

"MacGregor, is it?" Keir looked at him. "'Tis a bold lass who'll admit to the name in these times."

Better than telling you she's a Campbell. But he didn't say the words. "Her…da sent her this way." He ignored the look Charlotte gave him. It was true, in a way. She was *fleeing* from her father, according to her.

"For safety," Greer added quickly.

"There's that." Keir nodded. "Ye'll be safe enough among us. We've nae liking for the English telling us what to do, particularly in wantin' us to turn in our clansmen."

Charlotte smiled weakly. "That's good to know."

"How long will ye be staying?" Fiona asked.

It sounded like an innocent enough question, but Fiona's smile didn't quite reach her eyes. What she really meant was *When will Charlotte be leaving?*

Niall tried to mask his own expression. He'd made the mistake of kissing Fiona under the mistletoe at Yule. Even though she had maneuvered him into position, he couldn't say he hadn't gone along with it. The lass was comely. The kiss had been…interesting. Not interesting enough that he wanted to indulge further, even if his father thought it would be a good pairing. Besides, Keir was his friend who'd probably kill him if he didn't marry his sister. Unfortunately, Fiona was headstrong and had definitely let him know she was available for more sport. Her question was a loaded one.

"I'm not quite sure," Charlotte said.

"For awhile though," Greer said blithely, obviously unaware of the undercurrent. "There's still a risk to MacGregor women closer to the border."

Fiona smiled again, although to Niall it looked somewhat feral.

"Aye, I suppose ye wouldna want the mark on your face," she said to Charlotte.

"Of course she wouldn't!" Greer exclaimed. "What female would want to be branded because of her name?"

Niall thought Charlotte's color faded at that remark, and he wondered if she didn't know about the heinous procedure or if she had suddenly realized the danger of the name she'd assumed.

Keir was right, though. This far north, Scots weren't about to turn in one of their own to the English. Charlotte would be safe here.

However, the hair at his nape prickled when he saw Fiona was still studying Charlotte with an analytical look in her eye.

It seemed he was to play the valiant bodyguard after all.

Chapter Five

Charlotte tried not to be obvious about her eavesdropping on the conversation between Niall and his brother after dinner that night, but if she were going to be of any help at all in preventing the massacre at Culloden, she needed to gather as much information as she could and as unobtrusively as she could.

Luckily, the men had not retreated to the privacy of their council room—or the War Room, as she liked to call it. Instead, they were seated near her and Greer beside a roaring fire in one of the hearths in the Great Hall. The weather had turned surly after they returned from shopping in Inverness. The wind was howling and the snow was blowing in white-out conditions.

Somewhat like it would be on that fateful day just three and a half months hence.

"The missive Da received said General Murray decided to split the army into two parts on the advance to Stirling," Simon said. "I wonder how the prince is going to react to that."

"If he's wise, he'll listen to the man. He commands the Atholl Highlanders, and they are one of the strongest forces the prince has."

"Aye, but ye ken when Lord Murray returned from exile, he was appointed sheriff depute for the English before he crossed the line to us." Simon glanced over to where Charlotte sat. "And he approved the 1707 Union."

Charlotte pretended not to notice, but her ears burned and not because of the fire's heat. She was a Campbell and—in this time—a government ally, but she could hardly explain that she *wasn't* from this time.

"I doona think anyone will doubt his allegiance now," Niall said.

"Mayhap, but I wonder if his men are in agreement with dividing the army. The lord doesnae like to accept advice."

Niall shrugged. "He probably relies on his own experience, which is considerable."

"'Tis nae denying that, since he fought for the Old Pretender too." Simon grimaced. "but our bonny prince doesnae like to take orders either."

"Well, he *is* our prince," Greer interjected. "What do ye expect?"

Charlotte managed not to laugh at the surprised looks on her brothers' faces. They probably didn't think their sister had been listening to a word they said. She quickly straightened her own lips. *She* was probably not supposed to be listening either. Still, she glanced over at Niall, who seemed to have recovered from Greer's outburst.

"He may be our prince, but he is nae a seasoned warrior," he said.

Simon snorted. "He doesnae think things through, from what I heard. A bit of a hothead, he is."

Greer narrowed her eyes. "'Tis close to treason ye speak, brother."

"'Tis the truth."

Simon glanced her way again and Charlotte wondered if he'd made the statement on purpose to test her own reaction. Or…maybe feed her a tidbit that he might not be as strong a Jacobite as his brother and sister? Did he think her a spy, who would send a message to her "friends" to let them know? Or to that colonel at the fort?

She closed her eyes briefly and gave herself an inner shake. Her writer's imagination was taking over again. There was nothing nefarious about this conversation. They were simply discussing a decision that had been made by one of the top commanders of the Jacobite army. Plus, she *had* read that Bonnie Prince Charlie was stubborn and arrogant and young.

"However that may be," Niall said, "we doona ken if the prince agrees with Murray or not. We will have to wait and see."

That put an end to the conversation, but Charlotte kept the thoughts in her mind. A prince and a first-in-command at odds with each other did not bode well.

****

Two days later, they were back in Inverness, this time to check at the inns to see if her friends had either checked in or responded to the notices that had been left. Niall thought Charlotte appeared to be nervous, but whether that was because it was just the two of them today or because she anticipated—or *didn't* anticipate—news of her "friends."

He hated that he was still in doubt about her story. It didn't help that both Simon and his father were skeptical. While he could sympathize with a lass wanting to run away from a marriage she didn't want, it was very odd that her companions had not stuck around to find her. Then, too, there was the fact that she was a Campbell. He wouldn't put it past the Duke of Argyll to send a woman to infiltrate a Jacobite stronghold.

As bad as that possibility was, it would be even worse if Charlotte's nervousness was because she was alone with him this morning. Damn it. He *liked* the lass. He wanted her to trust him.

"Well, here we are," he said as they approached the first inn. "Let's see if your friends are about."

Charlotte gave him a wavering smile. "It would be wonderful to find them."

They had no luck there nor on the second or third stop. The wind had also picked up, and it was beginning to snow. Charlotte looked decidedly more anxious, but again, he didn't know if was the negative results they were having or because a storm was approaching.

"Maybe we should head back?" she asked.

"'Tis only five miles to home," Niall answered, "and we've got only a few more stops to make. Do ye nae want to check those first?" He hoped she would, since his father had given him an order to make sure all inns had been checked. Still, he would come back later if she wanted to go home. To his relief, she nodded.

"I suppose that would be best."

By the time they'd finished—with no luck—the storm had gathered strength and the snow fell more thickly. Niall thought about checking into a room—rooms—themselves to wait it out, but it seemed rather unnecessary, given how close they were to the castle and the horse knew well the way. Besides, he'd never hear the end of it from Simon if they stayed in town overnight. Or from his sister either, probably.

By the time they reached the stable where they'd left the horse and buggy, Charlotte had pulled her cloak tighter and wrapped the wool scarf more securely over her head and tugged on her gloves.

Niall hesitated. “We can get a room—rooms—and stay the night, if ye think ye’ll be too cold.”

Her eyes widened, whether in surprise or wariness he couldn’t tell. Then she shook her head.

“I’ll be fine. As you said, it’s only five miles.”

Niall asked the stable master for extra blankets. The man only had one on hand that wasn’t a horse blanket, so Niall laid it over Charlotte’s lap, tucking the edges in behind her, his hand brushing her side as he did so. It gave him an unexpected tingle.

Resisting the urge to tuck the whole blanket around her, he climbed up beside her on the bench and clicked the reins. As the horse moved outside, he felt her hand touching his thigh. He inhaled sharply, not daring to look at her. What was she doing? Not that he minded…she could stroke his whole leg if she wanted to. Warmth filled his nether regions at the thought. Then he felt a different kind of warmth and realized she had simply spread the blanket out to cover his legs as well. He did glance at her then and caught her watching him, a look of amusement on her face.

Amusement? Had the lass noticed his physical reaction? If she had, *amusement* wasn’t exactly the reaction he’d have hoped for.

But then again, she didn’t look afraid anymore.

****

More than anything, Charlotte wanted to move closer to Niall on the buggy’s bench. Not just for warmth, although that was definitely a factor since the temperature must have dropped a good ten or fifteen degrees, but she thought she’d felt a… *stirring*… when she’d placed the blanket over him. It would have been wonderful to test her theory by snuggling closer. Maybe he'd remember that kiss he'd given her on New Year's Eve.

She remembered it, although she wasn't sure if had been in the twenty-first century or this one. Niall seemed to have no recall of it at all. Which was a bit of a blow to her vanity. If it happened. Maybe it didn't. She'd been in this century only a few days, and her mind was still having trouble accepting reality. Whatever *reality* was. A now familiar, hysterical bubble rose in her throat. Her mind was used to operating in fantasy—that's what all writers did, especially romance writers—but this time she wasn't able to just shut the computer down. She was *here*. Wasn't she? A part of her wanted to take off her mittens and pinch herself to make sure she was not partaking of some very strange dream—like when she couldn't run—but it was getting colder by the minute. In spite of the blanket, she shivered.

Niall gave her a concerned look. "Are ye verra cold?"

"I…I'll be fine."

"Hmmph." He seemed to contemplate, then gave her a tentative smile. "If ye willna take offense at the suggestion, ye are welcome to sit on my lap and we'll wrap the blanket around both of us for body warmth."

Take offense? She fought down a giggle. Take offense? She'd been wanting to do that very thing, and not just for warmth. *Still*. She never allowed her heroines to throw themselves at their heroes. She furrowed her brows as if considering it, then nodded. "I think that would benefit both of us."

He made a noise low in his throat that was indecipherable although it came close to a growl. Then he wound the reins over the brake handle and lifted his half of the blanket.

It was a bit awkward trying to sidle over his thigh with all the winter clothing she was wearing and the narrow space. The heroines in her novels would have been able to do it gracefully in one smooth, sylph-like movement, but she got a corner of her cloak caught on the splintered wooden rail in front of the bench. When Niall reached around her back to untangle it, she stumped her foot against his boot just as the carriage lurched and she sprawled across his lap.

For a moment she lay there, hands clutching his leg, her head hanging over the side of the bench, the ground rising and falling beneath her face while the horse's trot had her jostling Niall. A certain part of him anyway.

He made another strange noise, and then she felt strong hands lifting her and settling her in a more dignified position against his chest. In another moment, he'd swirled the blanket around them, enveloping her in cocoon-like warmth. She was too embarrassed to look at him, so she just burrowed her head into the thick wool of his tartan.

Niall didn't speak either, which was just as well. What comment could he make after she'd so spectacularly completed such a klutz act? One that also had her in a very suggestive pose, to say the least. Instead, he unwound the reins with one hand and kept his other arm wrapped tightly around her shoulders, probably to make sure she didn't perform another artless blunder.

It did feel good to be held by him, though, even if he weren't aware of the wayward path her writer's imagination was taking her now that she was warm and safe, her senses filled with his scent of heather soap and leather.

She settled for curling her arms around his waist and felt his heart beating strong and steadily as she nestled against his chest. He was definitely *real*.

****

Niall had never been so glad to see the gates of Castle Dounie rising ahead of him through the swirling snow. It wasn't the weather that caused him concern—the horse instinctively knew the way to a warm barn and a waiting bucket of oats—but the lass he held in front of him.

Was God—or more likely, the devil—testing his limits? Sitting in close proximity to Charlotte on the buggy's bench had been temptation enough, or so he'd thought. Then she'd touched his leg when she'd covered them both with the blanket. Sharing that blanket, especially after her hand had unwittingly brushed against another part of him too, had felt instantly intimate. It was nothing to having her sprawled across him a moment later, soft, delectable breasts pressed against his rapidly rising member. He hadn't had that kind of lustful reaction since a cheeky milkmaid had pulled him into the straw when he was a lad.

And the worst part? Or—maybe—the best part…for her anyway. Charlotte seemed to be blissfully unaware, curled as she was against his chest, seemingly content, maybe asleep even. She trusted him and he had no right to take advantage of her. There were plenty of women he could have to meet his "needs," including Fiona.

Niall shook his head to clear his thoughts as the horse picked up his trot, sensing he was near home. Maybe these unforeseen emotions were surfacing because he'd not been with a woman in…months? Ever since Charles Edward John Sylvester Maria Casimir Stuart had arrived on Scotland's shores on July 23 with his ambition of reclaiming Scotland, Niall had been caught up in the Cause. Even now—this very day—fellow Highlanders were laying siege to Stirling.

Had Charlotte not literally fallen into his arms on Hogmanay, he'd probably be there too.

But she had fallen into his arms, and now she was in them again. She felt soft and pliable and molded to him flawlessly. He tried to push away the thought of how perfectly they'd fit together lying in his feather-down bed, the drapes from the canopy pulled closed, creating their own special cocoon, shutting away the rest of the world.

He sighed as he passed through the gates and entered the castle bailey. The world—his world—could not simply be vanquished because he would prefer to live in a time when Scotland wasn't at war.

Neither could he ignore the fact that the woman he held was an enigma as well. He glanced down at her nestled against him. Her assertion of fleeing a marriage she didn't want was plausible. Her account of her "friends" was highly suspicious. Did they exist? He'd not found any confirmation today that they had even been seen. But his da had not found any evidence that there were strangers lurking about, either.

Who was she, really? He was pretty sure she'd been truthful when she'd told him her name was Campbell. Who would pretend to be a member of a clan loyal to the government? That put her in danger in these parts, and he would protect and defend her for that reason alone. He was honor-bound. But if he thought his attraction to her wasn't real, that notion was gone.

Chapter Six

Charlotte meticulously cut a slice of venison on her plate and took her time buttering a bannock, averting her gaze as much as she could at dinner that evening. She still felt her cheeks warming every time she thought of herself sprawled over Niall's lap earlier and the reaction it had caused. *Especially* the reaction. Coming from the twenty-first century, she knew the swelling of his manhood had been only a physical reaction and not necessarily personal, but the response still excited her as well. If they were in the twenty-first century, she might well have encouraged him. Unfortunately, eighteenth-century morals were quite different if a female wanted to be considered respectable—and she needed to stay respectable, given her current situation.

Thea would no doubt scoff at her for caving, but Thea wasn't here. This afternoon's visits to the inns in Inverness had pretty much proved that neither Thea nor Vi was in this century. She was going to have to come up with some excuse as to why her friends were not looking for her. *Soon.*

"Ye had nae luck today?" Greer asked.

Charlotte shook her head. "None."

Greer looked at her brother. "Did ye check the ledgers?"

"There was nae need. The innkeepers had not seen them." Niall frowned. "Why do ye ask?"

"I was just thinking." She turned to Charlotte. "Your friends were a Sutherland and a Ross, nae?"

"Yes."

Greer turned back to Niall. "They might have used different last names since their clans are nae liked in these parts."

Niall's frown deepened while Charlotte felt a spark of hope, something akin to getting an inspirational plot point in one of her novels when she hit writer's block.

"I think the reason the innkeepers haven't seen them is because they're gone."

Four pairs of eyes riveted on her.

"Why would you say that?" Niall asked.

"Aye. Ye said they were your friends," Simon added.

"They were. Are. *Are* my friends," Geez, she'd almost blown it already, but her mind was still trying to spin the story. "But the intent was never to stay by my side forever, only to help me get away." She looked at Greer, since it was easier than meeting Niall's eyes. "Their families are like yours…they'll send out search parties if they were gone too long."

Simon raised a brow. "And your kin will nae come looking for ye?"

"I…suppose they might." Where was she going to go with this? The plot was getting messy. She began to feel desperate when ingenuity struck. Yes! "We each left a note for our families that we were going to celebrate Hogmanay in Glasgow."

"Glasgow?" Niall asked.

"Thea has relatives there." That much was true, but they were in the twenty-first century. "It wouldn't be that unusual for us to visit them." And they *had*, Thea and Vi and herself, before they'd come to Inverness. 270-plus years in the future.

The plotline of her story was growing. Maybe this tale would work. She prayed that it would. She allowed herself a tentative smile. "Besides, if my betrothed tries to find me, I want him heading in the opposite direction."

For a moment, amusement flickered in Niall's eyes, then faded. "Your betrothed…how determined will he be to find ye?"

"Ah…" Just who was her "betrothed"? She hadn't done a character sheet on him yet. "I'm not sure. He's…prideful."

Simon grimaced. "Just what we need. A bloody Campbell chasing after ye."

"He's not a Campbell." She spoke without thinking.

"Nae? Which clan, then?"

"Umm…" Think. *Think.* Her writer's mind went into overdrive. She had a cousin… "Grant. His name is Colin Grant."

Simon narrowed his eyes. "Which family does he belong to? George Grant or James?"

For a moment, Charlotte was nonplussed. How in the world could they know her uncle's name was George? Was her world changing back? But nothing moved and she didn't feel dizzy. "George."

Greer gasped. Simon swore. Their father banged his mug on the table. Luckily, it was pewter. Niall groaned.

Charlotte looked at them. Her blood felt like it was turning to ice by their expressions. "What? What is it?"

Niall looked at his father and brother, then turned to her. "General George Grant is nae our friend, lass."

"And he's a hell of a lot closer to us than the Campbells," Simon said.

Greer glared at him. "Must ye curse?"

Her brother glared back. "The clan holds Urquhart Castle, just fifteen miles from here."

"There's a wee bit of water in between." Niall looked at Charlotte. "If your betrothed lives that close, though, ye would have been smarter to go to Glasgow or Edinburgh."

Whoops. Had she blundered? "No. He doesn't live there." That was true. Her cousin had never been to Scotland. "He..." Good God. Where should he live? Where would be far enough away, yet close enough to the Campbell seat? Charlotte wished Thea was here. She knew her history. Wait, though...she did know of a place. "He lives at Fort William."

Simon's eyes were like twin blades of steel. "An *English* soldier."

For a moment, Charlotte wasn't sure how to answer. She certainly seemed to be putting her foot in her mouth. Or, maybe, since this was Scotland, she was putting both feet into boggy ground that would suck her under. *This is what happens when I don't outline a story.* But this was no time for self-recrimination. She was going to have to fly by the seat of her pants this once. And...maybe... Insight flared. "Yes. He is. He's a soldier. That's partially the reason I do not want to marry him." She looked again at Greer since she still didn't think she could meet Niall's gaze. "He's on the wrong side of the war. Just one reason I don't want to marry him."

Silence met that remark. Simon and his father exchanged glances. It seemed like an eternity before anyone spoke.

"Ye do have a point, lass," Niall said.

"I still doona like it," Simon growled.

Simon was beginning to irritate her. She was doing her best with this fabrication, although she didn't think anyone would appreciate the irony of it except her. She lifted her head and stared back. "I do not like it either, but it is what it is."

He was not cowed. Instead he narrowed his eyes. "I still doona believe your friends would have left ye."

"I already told you why they would have to leave," she shot back. "What else can I tell you?"

"Nothing more." Greer glared at her brother. "'Tis possible when her friends saw her with Niall, they kenned she would be in good hands and knew it would be safe to leave."

Charlotte managed to avoid gaping at her. That was a ploy worthy of a Regency heroine, although fifty years too early for this time.

"Enough of this talk," Niall said suddenly. "Greer speaks true. Frasers will protect those who want protection." He looked at Charlotte and his gaze softened. "And ye will have mine, lass. I swear it."

Charlotte swallowed hard, hoping she wouldn't succumb to actual swooning. Nothing in her novels could compare to the sincerity of the oath he had just given her. And she…she was a fraud.

****

Niall suspected Simon and his father were not happy with his avowal to protect Charlotte, and those suspicions were confirmed when he was summoned to the council room shortly after dinner. Both his sibling and his parent wore combative looks he knew only too well.

"Ye might as well have your say," he said as he

pulled out a chair and sank down on it.

Simon looked at their father, who gestured that he should begin. Turning to Niall, he looked ready to spit fire.

"'Tis bad enough we are housing a Campbell, but have ye gone completely barmy? She is betrothed to a *Grant*."

Niall shrugged. "One she says she doesna want to marry."

"A convenient story, mayhap," his father said.

"What do ye mean by that?"

"Deceiving ye by telling the tale and gaining your sympathy," his father replied, "to keep ye from discerning the real reason she is here."

If anyone knew anything about a thing or two about deception, it was his father. The man was an expert at it and equally expert at concealing it. Niall wasn't sure what his da's real motives were, but he needed to stand his ground.

"What do ye think the 'real' reason is, then?"

It was his father's turn to shrug. "Campbells and most Grants are allied with the government. Can ye nae figure it out for yourself?"

Niall ignored the bait. He also refrained from reminding his father that *he* had sided with the government to suit his own ends. "I believe the lass."

Simon waved a hand. "'Tis because ye want to tup her. Ye canna see what lies behind the bonnie looks."

"I doona want—"

"Aye, ye do. 'Tis written plainly on your face."

Niall scowled. He hated when his brother could read him, but he couldn't deny that lust served well as a distraction. Nor could he deny the feeling itself. He'd proved *that* just this afternoon. He squelched his anger—never an emotion to allow when he was about to do battle—and smiled at Simon.

"Since I am obviously a mooncalf in this situation, why do ye nae enlighten me as to how devious the lass is?"

Simon ignored his sarcasm. "Things do nae add up, brother. A bonnie lass just shows up and attaches herself to ye at Hogmanay. Then she swoons. Her 'friends' are nae to be seen. So ye bring her home—"

"What was I supposed to do? Leave her lying on the street?"

"Even today, ye could find nae clue that the 'friends' exist," Simon continued as though Niall hadn't interrupted, "and we couldna find hide nor hair of Campbells lurking about—"

"Which should prove to ye she is nae a spy," Niall said.

"On the contrary." This time, his father spoke. "She could be providing information to the colonel at the fort or in alliance with the Grants. One of them could be hiding in full sight in Inverness."

"What would be the logic in that if she is nae willing to *marry* a Grant?" Niall asked.

His father looked at him as though he'd gone daft. "What if the lass lies? What if, instead of running away from Colin Grant, he is really the person she reports to?"

"Urquhart is a half-day's ride from here, their clan seat less than twenty miles. If there is a Grant waiting close by, she could easily send a message to them about our plans for the Cause," Simon added.

"She has nae asked a single question."

"So far, she has nae had to," Simon said. "We

haven't mentioned where the prince is staying—so she has nae a thing to report. Yet."

"Yet?" As much as he didn't want to think such a thing was possible, Niall had to admit that everything his brother—and even his father—had laid out was a possibility. Wars had been lost, kingdoms had toppled, because men had been duped by women. He didn't like considering that his feelings for Charlotte would get in the way of his rational thinking, but the attraction was strong.

"Yet," Simon replied. "I ken ye want to protect the lass and—if she speaks true that she is running away from a Grant—I will support her as well."

Niall gave him a wary look. "And how do ye intend to prove she is telling the truth?"

"By feeding her lies." His father grinned.

"Which ye are an expert at." The words came out without thought, but Niall wasn't about to take them back.

His father didn't seem offended. "Mayhap it takes a liar to find a liar? I say we give the lass some *misinformation*—since ye doona like the other term—and see what she does with it."

"Aye." Simon nodded. "We ken that Murray split the army into two, one to distract while the other advanced to Stirling. We can tell her about the split but give alternative destinations." He grinned too. "That will benefit us twice over."

Niall narrowed his eyes. "What do ye plan to do?"

His brother's grin widened. "Play cat-and-mouse. We give her the information, then we announce a trip to Inverness where we men have to meet someone so she will be free do some shopping—"

"No woman can resist that," his father chortled.

Simon shook his head. "Beside the point, Da. It will give the lass an opportunity to relay her message. We will have her followed, of course. If she meets someone, we will ken she is a spy."

"I doona like it." Niall sighed. "But if it will keep ye from hammering on about it, I will nae stand in the way—"

"Good."

"—but ye said this would serve twice over. What do ye mean by that? I'll nae have Charlotte hurt, nae matter what the outcome."

"I wasn't speaking of hurting her," Simon glared at him. "I am nae a monster."

Niall glared back. "Then what did ye mean?"

"'Tis obvious, brother." His expression changed, and now he looked amused. "If the lass is a spy and gives out the wrong information, the government armies will be marching the wrong way. Murray will be able to declare victory without losing a single man because he won't be where the English think he is."

"Brilliant!" his father said.

Niall wasn't so sure, but at this point there was no use arguing.

However, he intended to not let Charlotte out of his sight when they were out. It was the one way he knew he could protect her.

And find out the truth.

Chapter Seven

Fraud. Charlotte didn't like the word. Much less did she want to apply it to herself. How else to describe, though, what she had been doing? Making excuses, fabricating stories, inventing people who didn't exist…

She looked around the table where they had just finished taking their noonday meal. Even if Simon and his father weren't exactly welcoming—and she understood their wariness, given the times and her name—they had still extended Highland hospitality and taken her in. Greer had accepted her and Niall had been… Well. Niall had every characteristic she'd ascribe to one of fictional heroes. Not only did he fit the physical description for a book cover—handsome, muscular, *sexy…he oozed masculinity*—but he also fit the attributes of a hero. He was protective, caring, concerned, and honorable.

He didn't deserve to be deceived. But she couldn't very well sit him down and tell him she was from the twenty-first century. She paused, her writer's imagination running away with her. *Could* she? Could she tell him? If she had proof? Maybe she needed to go back to the banks of River Ness and see if she could find some sort of portal. If she could show him a Time portal, maybe she could convince him of the massacre that was going to take place on April 16.

She gave herself an inward shake at being so absurd.

If she could find the Time portal—but if it truly wasn't Brigadoon descending once every hundred years, she would no doubt be cast as some sort of witch. And *that* would have dire consequences. She'd be joining the ranks of the deceased.

So, better to stick to the plot line she was manufacturing. At least, it was somewhat plausible. However, if Niall ever found out… She closed her eyes momentarily. She didn't want to go there. Couldn't go there.

"Are ye feeling ill, lass?" Niall asked.

She blinked. "I'm fine. My eyes were just burning." Another lie.

"Ye're sure ye weren't overcome by the conversation?" Simon asked. "Greer is used to it, but ye are nae from these parts."

Conversation? She hadn't been listening. "I—"

"Never ye mind," Greer interrupted. "It seems men canna stop talking about war and death."

"Death?"

"Numbers." Greer grimaced. "'Tis nothing to be proud of."

"Ye are nae proud that we kill King George's men rather than have them kill us?" Simon asked. "Ye doona think Lord Murray's rout at Stirling a success? That he can now advance on to Perth?"

Their father chuckled. "I would wager General Hawley will be a wee bit surprised when seven thousand Scots advance on him at Perth."

Simon nodded. "'Twould be a quick victor for us if Hawley doesna ken we are coming."

Greer rolled her eyes. "Can ye not think of something else to talk about?"

“Aye,” Niall said, his voice sounding hard. “I doona think Charlotte cares to hear about Scots’ war strategy.”

His father gave him a level look, one that Charlotte couldn’t decipher but instinctively felt was some sort of unspoken message. Simon, too, was practically boring a hole into Niall with his stare. Maybe she had missed something important. If she were going to be any help at all in this century, she would have to start paying attention to which battles the Scots were engaging in and where.

They’d been talking about death? What they didn’t know was how many of them would die at Culloden if she couldn’t prevent that battle from happening.

****

Fate did indeed work in mysterious ways. For the past few days, Charlotte had pondered a way to get back to Inverness and be able to revisit the area near the river where she had last been in the twenty-first century. If she found a portal, maybe then she could convince Niall she knew the Scots would be defeated by the English if they continued their Cause because she knew the outcome.

The opportunity had presented yesterday when Niall’s father announced they’d be going into the city this morning and asked if she’d like to come along. Greer had gone into Beauly for her weekly meeting with the local vicar to see which neighbors might be in need of help, so Charlotte was left at odds.

“You’re awfully quiet this morning,” she said to Niall a short time later after they’d settled in the carriage and the driver had put the horses to a brisk trot.

“My brother broods a lot,” Simon said from the seat facing them. “Pay him nae mind.”

In the little over a week that she’d been with the

Frasers, she didn't think Niall was the broody sort, although right now he gave his brother a dark look.

"I have a problem—not of my own making—that I need to solve," he said.

"The problem is *ours* to solve," his father said.

"Can I help?" Charlotte could have sworn Simon started to grin but quickly sobered when Niall glared at him. Their father guffawed loudly.

"'Tis a family matter," Niall said between clenched teeth. "A wee bit of an argument we had earlier."

"Oh." She wasn't quite sure what else to say. "I…didn't mean to intrude."

"Intrude? That's an interesting word choice," Simon said.

Charlotte furrowed her brow. "It is? I just meant I don't want to interfere with your lives."

"Ye are nae interfering, lass."

The look Niall gave his brother was one Charlotte couldn't decipher, but a message was definitely being relayed. Was it a warning? Maybe he was telling his brother to say no more because it was a personal matter that Niall didn't want her to know about. She didn't need to pry.

They rode in mostly silence the rest of the short distance. When they alighted from the carriage, she was expecting Niall would accompany her since he had other times when they'd left the castle, so she was surprised to hear his father speak.

"If ye doona mind, Miss…MacGregor, the lads and I need to meet with our solicitor. Can ye manage by yourself for an hour or so?"

Fate certainly seemed to be doing her all sorts of favors today. "Of course. I'll not wander far."

Niall opened his mouth, about to say something, when Simon nudged him. "Come along, brother. Ye ken we shouldna be late for our appointment."

He hesitated a moment, then nodded. "We willna be long, lass."

"An hour," Simon countered. "At least."

"Do not worry," Charlotte answered. "I can manage by myself."

Niall gave her another look she couldn't decipher, then followed his brother and father. She watched them until they disappeared around a corner onto a side street and then turned back to the river. She shaded her face with her hand to avoid the glare of the water and squinted, not sure what she was looking for. Some sort of mist hovering? Maybe an unusual light effect? No, that would be too obvious. Besides, she hadn't gone into the river.

She chided herself for being so silly and walked to the spot where she had stood before joining the dancers. The ground felt solid. Her surroundings didn't shimmer. There were no tiny light specks dancing in the air like faeries. *Stop that!* Her writer's imagination was running amok again. She wasn't writing a story about Scottish folklore, for heaven's sake, or a passage to the Otherworld. She was looking for a *real* portal, one that she had somehow moved through. But where was it? She glanced around, looking at the area where the stranger had appeared to Vi and then over to the place where Thea had gone to help the fallen man. Nothing but ordinary people going about their daily business.

She made her way down closer to the river, where the dancing had taken place. She'd already covered this area before, but she'd been in the company of the Frasers and she could have missed something. This time, she paused every few feet to look around and tried to sense anything "different" but all seemed normal. Sighing, she sat down on a bench on the river bank to contemplate.

"Do ye mind if I share the bench for a minute or two?"

Startled, Charlotte looked around to see a young, auburn-haired woman about her own age smiling at her. She wore a simple dress of pale blue wool with a darker sash and no apron, so Charlotte assumed she probably worked in one of the shops. Maybe taking a break. She looked vaguely familiar, but Charlotte couldn't place her. She indicated the open space beside her. "Certainly. Please sit."

"Thank ye. This is a favorite spot of mine." The girl sat. "My name is Bridgid."

"I'm Charlotte."

Bridgid inclined her head and then gave her a curious look. "If ye'll forgive me for asking, I saw ye stop several times on your way over. Are ye looking for something?"

Well, yes. A passageway to the twenty-first century. Would you know where it is? Charlotte felt a by-now frequent bubble of hysteria trying to rise in her throat and swallowed hard. If she had been watched, maybe she should come up with some sort of excuse. "I…thought I'd dropped a trinket last time I was here."

"When was that?"

"Ah… Hogmanay, actually." She waved her hand. "I'm sure it's long gone by now, but I thought I'd look anyway."

"Hogmanay." The girl smiled again. "'Tis always a special time for gift-giving. Mayhap ye did someone a good turn."

"I hadn't thought of it that way." Although the girl couldn't possibly know, perhaps traveling through Time had been a gift after all. Charlotte smiled back. "I hope the trinket is in good hands then."

"I have a feeling it is." The girl stood. "I'd best be on my way then."

Charlotte nodded. "I'm glad you came by."

"Aye, 'tis always good to sit and reflect by the water." She inclined her head and then walked away.

Charlotte turned back to the water. Reflection was a good idea. Maybe she hadn't lied after all. Maybe *she* was the trinket that had been lost or found and was now in the hands of Niall Fraser.

****

Niall felt like a complete eejit hidden in the alleyway across from the river's bank, watching Charlotte. While he had done his share of lurking behind things in order to be privy to Government conversations, he didn't like spying on the lass.

"I hope ye both will be satisfied when we're done with this," he told his father and brother, who stood behind him. "'Tis shameful what we're doing."

"Ye willna say that if it turns out she has an accomplice in Inverness," his father said.

"Aye, and if she puts Frasers in danger," Simon added.

Niall grunted. "She has nae done anything with the lie ye told her about our men moving toward Perth."

"When has she had the opportunity before today?" his father asked.

"My point exactly," Niall responded. "If she truly were sent by the colonel or other Campbells or Grants, she would have made some excuse to get to Inverness to relay the information to her courier as quickly as possible."

"That might make her look suspicious," Simon said. "She would know she had a bit of time to relay the message since it takes an army days to travel."

His father nodded. "Aye. 'Twould be devious of her."

If anyone knew about being devious, it was his father, but Niall bit back the words.

"She's looking for someone," Simon said, interrupting his thoughts.

Niall turned back to see what his brother was talking about. Charlotte stood not far from where they'd left her, her hand raised over her eyes as she scanned the street. "Mayhap she is just trying to get her bearings to decide which way to go."

"Or she's looking for someone."

Sometimes his brother could be really pigheaded. Niall glowered at him. "Ye've already said that. 'Tis nae harm in looking about."

"*Now* what is she doing?" his father asked.

He turned back again and then furrowed his brows as he watched. Charlotte had started walking toward the river rather than to the shops. She was also stopping every few steps to look around.

"She's looking for someone," Simon said again.

Niall resisted the urge to plant his fist in his brother's face. "It seems to me she's looking at the ground, ye eejit."

Simon considered. "Mayhap she's hoping her henchman will find her if she lingers by the river. It's crowded along the street."

Niall took a deep breath. He supposed he shouldn't entirely blame Simon for his scrutiny. He had trained with their uncle Charles of Inverallochy and, as the older brother, would be the one to lead the Lovat Frasers when they were called on by the prince. Niall would join them, but as the second son, he wouldn't be the one making decisions.

Charlotte had taken a seat on a bench by the river and was gazing over the water. "It seems to me the lass is just relaxing."

"Hmmm." Simon came alongside him and then perked up, rather like a pointer dog finding a bevy of quail. "Someone is approaching her."

"Aye. A woman," Niall said dryly. "Do ye suspect her too?"

Instead of answering, Simon focused. Their father took another step forward as well. Niall frowned at both of them and then watched as the other woman sat down on the bench and began to talk with Charlotte. They were too far away to hear what was being said, of course, but it seemed like normal conversation to him. It didn't take long, though, before the other woman got up and left.

Simon turned to their father. "What do ye think, Da?"

The older man narrowed his eyes. "I think we need to find out who the other lass is."

"I agree. I'll follow her." Simon gave Niall a quick look and then was gone.

Niall sighed. "Da. Ye doona actually think that other woman is a spy?"

His father shrugged. "Why nae? If the Campbells sent a lass to spy for them, why nae have her accomplice be a female too?"

He practically sputtered. "'Tis ridiculous."

His father turned his full attention on Niall. "Is it, son? Think on it. The lass swoons in your arms. Ye bring her home. Her story is that two of her *women* friends helped her escape a marriage she doesna want. 'Tis very odd that her friends would just abandon her. We have nae been able to find those women." He paused. "Mayhap that was one of them."

"I doona think—"

"Precisely, son. Ye doona think." His father smirked. "At least, nae with the head that is on your shoulders."

Niall opened his mouth to respond, then clamped it shut. He didn't want to get into that discussion.

Apparently, his father did. "Ye are besotted with the Campbell lass and ye canna think straight."

"I am nae besotted!"

"Mayhap ye should just tup her and have it over with," he continued as if he hadn't spoken.

Somehow, Niall managed not to strike his father. "I willna take advantage of her."

His father shook his head. "Ye always were too damn honorable."

He bristled. "I didna ken that was a bad thing to be."

"To a degree. The lass poses a danger if ye canna keep your thinking straight." His father eyed him. "Remember Samson and Delilah?"

"Charlotte is nae Delilah."

"But are ye as trusting as Samson?"

Niall wasn't about to get into a Biblical discussion. "So what are ye really saying, Da? That ye want to turn Charlotte out on the streets? I'll nae agree."

The older man grinned. "Ye are only proving my

point that ye are besotted with the girl." His expression turned thoughtful as he looked back to where Charlotte was still sitting. "However, I agree we need to keep the lass with us. If she is a spy, we'll learn it soon enough." He turned to leave. "And then we can use her."

Naill watched his father walk away, not liking either what he'd said or the tone he'd used. He was all too aware of how his father "used" people. He wouldn't let that happen to Charlotte. He stepped out from the alley into the sunshine and started to make his way to Charlotte.

When they got home, Simon would have found out who the other woman was and that would be the end to this spy nonsense. No more questions or suspicion.

And he was not besotted. He was *not*.

****

The short ride back to Castle Dounie felt like a journey of a hundred miles. Charlotte had been quiet as if reflecting on something. Niall wanted to ask what that "something" was, just to assure himself it had nothing to do with the conversation she'd had with the young woman on the bench. Charlotte hadn't even mentioned the incident, which he wasn't sure was a good thing or a bad thing.

Then there was his brother. He'd been grim and tight-lipped ever since he'd met them at the carriage for the ride home. Niall couldn't decipher the reason, either. If Simon had discovered that the young woman had turned out to be a Campbell or a Grant, wouldn't he have looked happy that he *might* be right about her being a messenger? His dour expression also could be because he'd been *wrong*. In which case, Niall would tell him—and their father—that he wanted to hear no more accusations against Charlotte.

The midday meal was ready when they got home, so Niall had to wait an agonizing additional hour while they ate and Greer filled them in on which neighbors were having problems. Then a missive arrived letting their father know that the siege at Stirling had been partially successful—the town had surrendered, but the castle remained in English hands. They'd retreated to the council room to discuss the implications of that, which took another hour. Finally, after the Fraser man who'd brought the missive left, Niall turned to his brother.

"What did ye find out this morn?"

"Nothing."

"Nothing?" Of all the responses from Simon that Niall had mulled over, he'd not considered that one. "What do ye mean, nothing?"

"I couldna find the girl."

"Ye couldna find—" Naill changed to a question. "How could ye nae find her? She was nae that far ahead of ye."

Simon scowled at him. "When I got to the corner and turned, she was gone."

"Gone?" He was beginning to sound like a parrot, but he couldn't help himself. "What do ye mean, *gone*?"

"Gone." Simon's scowl deepened. "G-O-N-E. Vanished. Not anywhere to be seen. Do ye get the meaning?"

"I ken what 'gone' means, brother." Niall frowned. "How could ye lose her? 'Tis nae market day. The streets were nae that crowded. Did ye look into the shops?"

"Do ye think me daft? Of course I did."

"She couldna just have vanished."

"She might have," their father said, "if she had

someone waiting to sprint her away."

"Aye, I thought of that," Simon said. "It would make sense if she were waiting for Charlotte to appear."

Niall managed—just barely—to keep from swearing at both of them. "I think ye are both barmy, but for the sake of argument… How would the woman know that Charlotte would be coming into Inverness?"

"We told the lass yesterday that we would be going in this morning," his father answered. "That would give her ample time to send a message."

Niall couldn't believe his ears. "With whom, Da?"

His father shrugged. "A stable lad, most likely, but it could be just about any of the green lads that work here. She's quite bonnie."

Simon snickered. "Aye. They all do eye her when she walks by."

His blood stirred slightly and he felt a momentary pang of…jealousy?. He *had* noticed the lads acted like mooncalves around Charlotte, and he didn't much like the fact that they did, but he'd never seen her taking notice or interacting with any of them. He'd not seen cause to worry. Certainly not to be jealous, for God's sake. He wasn't. He was just reacting to his brother's ridiculous prattle.

"Ye are fabricating stories out of thin air."

"Mayhap," Simon said, "but even if she didn't sent a message, a courier would ken to wait until she showed up. They'd agree to a designated spot where the courier could blend in and it would not seem out of the ordinary to meet."

"Like the shopping area where women go all the time," his father added, "and then the bench at the riverside. No attention would be drawn to one woman talking to another while taking in the view."

"I think both of ye are letting your imaginations go wild," Niall said. "Neither of ye have any proof."

"Did ye notice that Charlotte nae mentioned the meeting?" Simon asked.

"She probably didna think it important."

"Or she hoped no one had seen her."

"How did the other woman just disappear if someone were nae waiting to whisk her away once she had a message to convey?" his father asked. "And, remember, we deliberately fed information to Charlotte so there would be a message to deliver."

Simon looked at Niall, not without sympathy for once. "The logical conclusion, brother, is that the English have planted a spy in our midst."

Their father nodded in agreement. "And the best way to keep an eye on a spy is to keep her nearby." He grinned suddenly. "That rhymed."

"Do ye think this is a game, Da?"

"Nae." His father sobered. "But if the lass has been sent to relay information about our plans, then we need to let her do that. With the wrong information, of course."

Niall clamped his mouth shut and didn't answer. He didn't want to believe that Charlotte was a spy. *Wouldn't* believe it. It couldn't be.

Chapter Eight

"Ye want to do what?"

Charlotte was tempted to laugh—or at least smile—at Niall's befuddled expression. However decorum was probably the better path to take at the moment. She'd asked to have a word with him in the study after dinner that evening.

"I said I would like to seek employment."

"Why?"

He sounded curious, which probably wasn't so odd since most women in the 18th century didn't go looking for work if they didn't have to. But that was her point. Earlier this afternoon, his father had found her with Greer in the solar and said it was good for his daughter to have female company and that he'd like to extend the invitation to Charlotte to stay for as long as she needed to. The invitation was a relief and also coincided with her plans to try to divert—somehow—the battle at Culloden. She did not intend to be a freeloader though.

"Since your father offered me lodgings, I want to earn my keep."

"Ye are a guest."

"I don't want to take advantage of that. You know the old adage about a three-day limit on fish and guests."

'What?"

This time he looked completely bewildered and she realized that old adage probably wasn't *that* old. "Never mind. I just meant that guests can become burdens if they aren't pulling their own weight."

He widened his eyes. "Ye want to drag something around that weighs what ye do? 'Tis a strange request."

"No." She really needed to stop with the idioms. "I meant, I want to contribute something. To be of some use."

"Ye can accompany Greer with her charity work, then."

"I can. I will. But I also need to earn some coin. I never did find my purse, and I can't stay here forever."

"Where would ye want to go?"

She hadn't given it much thought since she was still trying to figure out how she'd arrived here in the first place, but Niall was waiting for an answer.

"I'm not sure. Maybe the Colonies?" She'd come from the States, after all.

Several expressions crossed his face at once, each too fleeting for her to grasp. Was he realizing the practicality of what she was asking? Or was he reacting to her statement about not staying forever? Was he hoping she would? She almost laughed again. That was her romance writer self wishfully hoping. Niall had been nothing but kind and a perfect gentleman. Drat it. If she wanted proof of that, she only needed to remind herself that he didn't even *remember* the kiss on Hogmanay, although she could recall it in stark detail. She shook her head to clear it.

"'Tis a long way. Ye'd need much coin."

His tone was neutral and his expression passive. She couldn't tell what he was really thinking. Better not to pursue it, since she really didn't want to end up in colonial America.

"I was hoping I could perhaps work in a shop in Inverness."

His expression changed again, but this time he looked…suspicious? "In Inverness?"

"Well…yes. I doubt there is much opportunity for a woman to get a job in Beauly, since it's so small."

"Hmmm." He leaned back in his chair. "And how do ye plan to get there?"

"I can ride." Remembering what century she was in, she quickly added, "Sidesaddle, of course." She'd never ridden sidesaddle, but it couldn't be *too* hard.

One brow lifted. "We've a war going on. The roads are nae safe for a single lass."

"I could wrap one of your great plaids around me and put my hair up under a cap. No one would recognize I was a woman."

Both brows lifted at that and a corner of his mouth quirked up. "I doona think 'tis enough wool in Scotland to hide that fact."

She blinked. Was Niall flirting? Before she could think of a witty—maybe flirty—comeback, he added, "Besides, ye'd be riding sidesaddle."

So much for flirting, then. "I could ride astride if I had enough material covering me. No one would see my skirts."

His lips quivered as though he were trying hard not to laugh, and an assortment of changes crossed his face. For a brief moment, she wondered if she'd said *lift* my skirts rather than *see* my skirts. No. *No*, she hadn't.

"Do ye ken what ye'd look like? Some enterprising soul might think a wool merchant's horse wandered away and he'd take advantage of that, only to find ye in the midst of the load."

So he'd been trying not to laugh, picturing her as big bag of wool wandering down the road. Skirt-lifting hadn't even been on his mind. She sighed and rose from her seat. The conversation was not going in the right direction. *Either* direction—she wasn't winning her case about getting a job and she certainly wasn't making any headway in the flirtation department.

"Would you at least think about my request? I would really like to earn some money and feel useful."

He considered for what seemed like a short eternity and then nodded. "I'll think on it."

"Thank you." She walked to the door and glanced back, only to find him studying her with narrowed eyes, his sense of amusement gone.

She hurried away. Better not to question why.

****

"I told ye so."

Niall caught himself from telling his father to go to hell. Which was probably where he was headed without any help from himself. He sighed.

"Just because the lass wants to earn coin doesna mean she is a spy."

"I'm inclined to agree with Da," Simon said. "It looks suspicious."

Not surprising. Niall had hesitated to tell his father and brother about the conversation with Charlotte, but he doubted she was going to drop the issue, so he'd have to tell them anyway. Still, he'd slept on the matter before asking them to meet in the council room after breaking their fast this morning. Now, he wasn't so sure it had been the right choice after all.

"Do the two of ye nae think her reasoning was sound? That she wants to contribute to the family?"

"We doona need the money," his father said.

"And 'twould be an insult to us Frasers if anyone in Beauly thought we were making a guest—and a female one at that—go into the labor market," Simon added.

"She probably kens that, since she said Beauly was too small," Niall replied. "Nae one would ken her situation in Inverness, since it's bigger."

"And easier to meet up with her messenger," his father said.

Sometimes Niall felt like he was sitting on a spinning top when he spoke to his father. The man talked in circles. Maybe it was time to throw some words back at him.

"Did ye nae say ye wanted Charlotte to stay here so ye could observe her when she goes into Inverness?"

His father snorted. "Hard to observe her if she's there every day. We canna waste that kind of time following her when we have troops to ready."

"I—"

"Wait." Simon held up a hand. ."I think I have a solution."

Niall eyed him warily. "What is it?"

"The lass says she wants—for whatever reason—to earn coin. Mayhap she could work for Fergus Gordon."

"Our solicitor?" their father asked.

"Aye. Both his clerks joined Murray's forces at Stirling, so he'll be in need of someone to scribe and take care of paperwork.."

"Keir is working for him now," Niall said. "He didna say he needed help."

"Hmmm." His father ignored him and tented his hands. "That might work. Fergus could keep an eye on her and report any odd comings and goings."

Simon nodded. "And, if she leaves the office, Keir can follow her and let us know where she goes."

Niall narrowed his eyes. "Ye would tell them ye think Charlotte is a spy?"

His father shrugged. "Do ye nae think they should ken?"

"I doona." Niall shook his head. "Ye could verra well damage Charlotte's reputation when she doesna deserve it."

"And if she does?" his father countered. "Spies doona deserve mercy."

"Ye have nae proof she is!"

His father chuckled. "Which is why we set the trap."

"I willna agree to it." Niall frowned. "We can find another place for her to earn some coin."

Simon looked at him. "Where else in Inverness would she be as safe? At least, Fergus would nae mistreat her."

His brother did have a point. If Charlotte insisted on earning coin, their solictor's office would be a good place to do it. Women were vulnerable, even in respected shops sometimes. Still. Something niggled at him, but he wasn't sure what it was.

His father declared, "I still think we should tell Fergus everything."

"Nae!" Niall managed to keep his voice down. "I willna agree."

"Ye—"

"Wait," Simon interrupted again. "Niall may have a point, Da. If we let on we think the lass is a spy, she'll be watched *too* closely. And ye ken what a stickler Keir's father is for details. Ye'll nae hear the end of it from Fergus for taking such a risk by having her here."

"Now *there* is a truth," Niall said.

His father's expression darkened. "Then what do ye propose we tell him?"

"I think we can tell both Keir and his father *another* truth." Simon looked at Niall and grinned suddenly. "My brother is besotted with the lass. Since Keir is a good friend, we can tell him Niall wants the lass followed to make sure she's nae meeting another swain."

Niall felt his face grow hot. "I am nae besotted!"

"Your face tells another story." Simon's grin faded. "Or we could go with Da's idea and let them know what we suspect."

Niall scowled. "'Twould nae be fair to the lass."

"Then tell Keir to keep a watchful eye on her, brother." Simon's mouth quirked up. "If ye doona want to admit to being besotted, ye can at least say ye are interested, nae?"

Niall opened his mouth, then clamped it shut. This was not an argument he was gong to win. He sighed. "If Fergus accepts her, I will talk to Keir."

"Good." Simon glanced at their father and then turned back to Niall. "I'll write the letter of inquiry this morning."

Better Simon than their father. Niall nodded and then stood to leave. He was halfway down the hall when he realized what had been niggling at him.

Fergus Gordon was Fiona's father too.

Chapter Nine

Being summoned to the study was beginning to feel a little less like being called to the principal's office each time she went, although she was still wary. It had been several days since she'd had her conversation with Niall about finding work, so she assumed that this afternoon she would be getting her answer.

He was sitting in one of the armchairs by the hearth instead of behind the big desk, so hopefully that bode well for her. Or maybe he just wanted to put her at ease before he gave her the bad news. She hated having the decision as to whether she could work or not rest in someone else's hands—Vi would have a fit—but considering her unusual circumstances, which included being in the eighteenth century and not the twenty-first, she had little choice.

"You asked to see me?"

He rose and gestured her in. "Please. Have a seat."

Niall really would have made an excellent poker player, she decided, since nothing in his facial expression gave any indication as to where this conversation would go.

She sat. So did he. Good for starters.

He cleared his throat. "Tell me again why ye wish to secure employment."

What? Were they going to have this conversation again? She managed to keep from sighing. "I do not like having to be dependent on your family."

He studied her. "Ye are nae liking Castle Dounie?"

"No. I mean, yes. I mean…" She did sigh then. "Castle Dounie is fine. I cannot complain."

"Then ye wish to stay?"

She was getting confused by the line of questioning. However, given that she literally had no other place to go, she needed to be careful that she didn't get herself kicked out. "Of course, I would like to stay. I just… If I go to work, I can be helpful to you."

He turned. "What do ye consider being helpful?"

She furrowed her brows. "What do you mean?"

"Helpful," he said again, his gaze not leaving hers. "How do ye think having employment will be helpful?"

"Besides earning coin for myself, if I'm in Inverness several days a week, I may hear something about what the government is planning to do. I can then relate that to you."

Niall stared at her for a moment longer, then rose and walked to the window. The sunlight streaming through gave an almost bluish sheen to his hair and cast half of his strong, angular features in shadow. From the part she could see, he appeared to be troubled. Charlotte wasn't sure why, but something compelled her to rise and go to him. Standing this close, she caught the faint scent of soap and leather. She tried not to inhale too deeply as he gave her a glance.

"What is it? You look upset."

He didn't answer immediately, just turned and looked back out the window. It took restraint on her part not to tug on his arm and demand an answer, but somehow she managed to remain silent.

Finally, he looked at her. Another moment went by.

Still he hesitated, then sighed before he spoke.

'Verra well. Da talked to Fergus Gordon, our solicitor. He is in need of a clerk right now and agreed he'd take ye on—"

"Yes!" Restraint gave way to impulse. Charlotte raised on tiptoe and threw her arms around Niall's neck. "Thank you!" She turned slightly to kiss his cheek, only her aim was off, because she caught the corner of his mouth instead.

For an instant, he stood stock still. Then she felt his arms go around her waist as he gathered her close, his mouth finding hers. Time stood still. There was only the wonderful sensation of his lips sweeping across hers, gentle yet commanding. Skillful, just like she remembered…

"Oh, I'm sorry!"

The sound of Greer's voice from the doorway made Charlotte jump back while Niall slowly dropped his arms, his eyes lingering on her mouth long enough for her to grow increasingly warm. Then he looked to his sister.

"Can ye nae knock?"

"Why should I? I came for a book. I didna ken ye were…" She shrugged. "Well, ye can thank me later."

His eyebrows rose. "*Thank* ye?"

"Aye," Greer replied smugly. "Simon and Da are on their way."

****

Both Charlotte and his sister left before Simon and his father got there, which was lucky for Niall. Lucky because he knew his sister wouldn't be able to keep from smirking and his brother would be sure to pick up on it. And lucky, too, that Charlotte wasn't here. He didn't think he could keep a very self-satisfied smirk off his own face if she was.

Charlotte had kissed him. *She* had kissed *him*. Ever since he'd brought her home, he'd been wanting to taste her, feel her lips moving against his, have her open her mouth to him. She had been willing. He could feel it, not only because she'd thrown her arms around him, but the way her body melded easily into his, the way she had subtly pressed the softness of her plump breasts against his chest. If only Greer hadn't interrupted…

"Well, what did the lass say?" his father asked.

Niall pulled himself abruptly out of his fantasy of where that kiss might have led. And, he reminded himself sternly, if Greer *hadn't* come in when she did, his father and brother would have witnessed where that kiss might have led, which would have been disastrous…and not only because they thought he was besotted. Simon would have told him she was manipulating him, while his father would probably make another reference to Samson and Delilah.

"She was verra glad to hear it."

"Nae doubt," Simon said. "'Tis a good opportunity for her."

"And one that we'll be watching." His father eyed him. "Ye did explain the circumstances to Keir?"

"Aye. We had a talk." He made an effort to keep his expression impassive. Keir had laughed when he'd "admitted" he was interested in the lass and wanted to find out if she might have another swain. His friend would laugh even harder now that it was actually true. One kiss and he was already wondering if there had been other men in her life other than the betrothed Grant, whom she was running away from. "Keir kens what he needs to do, but I did swear him to secrecy."

"I still think it would be better if Fergus were aware," his father said. "We'd find out faster if she is a spy if she were fed incorrect information that she'd want to give to her messenger."

"We've already had this conversation, Da," Niall replied.

"I agree," Simon said unexpectedly. "The fewer people that ken what our suspicions are, the better. If she proves to be a traitor, we can claim we were nae aware."

His father looked thoughtful. "Aye. I suppose there is that. We wouldna want to be accused of knowingly harboring a government spy."

Simon nodded. "'Tis best, I think."

His brother could be almost as devious as his father at times, but Niall wasn't sure if he should be irritated with Simon's "logic" at the moment or whether to thank him for stilling their father.

"I also want to remind ye both that ye are on a fishing expedition here," Niall said. "Charlotte has told us she is running away from a marriage she doesna want. 'Tis common enough. Why should we nae believe her?"

"She could be trying to gain sympathy," his father answered. "Women are like that. Unscrupulous."

Niall would have laughed at the irony of his father saying that, but he was too annoyed. "Charlotte has told us she is a Campbell. Why would she do that if she were a spy?"

"Could be another ploy." His father shrugged. "Sometimes, the best thing to do is use the truth to deceive or divert the enemy."

Well, the Fox would know, although Niall did not think Charlotte was an enemy, especially after that kiss.

However, perhaps it would be best not to tell his father that Charlotte had offered to bring them information.

****

Charlotte avoided Greer's gaze as they left the study and made their way toward the stairs that led to the solar. She'd just been caught kissing Greer's brother. What could she say?

She stifled a sigh. Here she was—a twenty-first-century woman who was not a virgin—embarrassed about a kiss? Maybe the old adage about "when in Rome…" really did apply. Being caught kissing in the eighteenth century was probably akin to being caught *in flagrante delicto.*

Warmth spread through her as she recalled how sensuous the kiss had been, how wonderful Niall's arms felt pulling her close, how fantastically the two of them fit together as though made for one another. If only they hadn't been interrupted…

Something poked her. For a moment, still lost in her fantasy, she thought it might be him. Then she realized it was Greer's elbow instead. She was glad the hallway was lit only by sconces. Her face was probably flaming.

"Are ye back among us mortals?" Greer asked with a grin.

"What? I—" Her face definitely was on fire. "Yes, of course. Why?"

The stupid question was out before she could stop herself. She didn't need an answer. She knew why. Greer probably did too, although that didn't stop her.

"Ye look like ye are far, far away from here."

If Niall's sister only knew how far away from *here* she really was…

"Or," Greer continued, her grin widening, "maybe just downstairs in the study?"

That was exactly where she had been, still wrapped in an ever-deepening kiss, although she'd never admit it. "I suppose I should explain—"

"No need," Greer said. "I ken my brother. He's had his eye on ye since he brought ye home."

That sounded rather like she was a rescue puppy, but the other point... He was interested? "He has?" she asked. "Really?"

"Och, aye." Greer waved a dismissive hand. "He has always had an eye for a bonnie lass."

Well. That statement was certainly an ego-deflator. Although not so different, either, from twenty-first-century men. That wasn't anything new, merely human nature. She grimaced. *Still.*

Greer frowned slightly. "Did he take advantage of ye?"

"What? No. *No.*" Greer shook her head. She certainly couldn't *blame* Niall since she was the one who instigated the whole thing. Probably best not to admit that, though, since she didn't know how Greer would take it. "I...didn't mind."

The frown was replaced by a smile. "It didna look like ye did, but I wanted to make sure my brother was nae giving ye unwanted attentions."

A giggle threatened to burst out, but she managed to push it down. "He wasn't. It...just happened. I was...just happy to hear I could work in Inverness." She looked at Greer. "Maybe it would be better if you didn't mention what happened to Simon or your father?"

"Doona fash. My lips are sealed." Greer studied her for a moment. "But ye might do well to have a care around the two of them. Especially Da." She hesitated. "He wants Niall to marry Fiona Gordon. He will nae take it kindly if he thinks ye are interfering."

Charlotte felt like one of the castle's horses had kicked her solidly in the stomach. Marriage plans? That had not occurred to her. Did Niall agree? It probably didn't matter if he did, given that many—most—marriages in the eighteenth century weren't based on love but on logical reasons like alliances and land and power. Her romance-writing mind had forgotten that.

She swallowed hard. "Thank you. I'll remember."

She needed also to remember that getting attention from Niall—however wonderful it felt—didn't define his intention. Women who casually involved themselves in trysts were not held in much respect. She would have laughed if she didn't feel so much like crying.

The eighteenth century wasn't so different from the twenty-first after all.

Chapter Ten

"I would like to introduce Miss MacGregor to ye," Niall said formally the next morning when they arrived at the family solicitor's office.

The man he introduced her to was perhaps just past middle age. He had a full head of caramel-brown hair that showed silver tips on his sideburns. He was also physically fit, not soft or pudgy as she would have expected for someone who spent most of his time in an office or at a desk in this century. Then again, life was neither luxurious or easy in these times.

The older man smiled. It was not a particularly warm smile and didn't reach his eyes, but it didn't seem forced, either. Professional, maybe. Somewhat like her college professors had used when welcoming students to a new semester. Approachable, but also aloof.

"I am pleased to make your acquaintance," she said.

"Likewise," he returned although he didn't offer his hand. "I am Fergus Gordon."

Gordon? The family solicitor's name was Gordon? As in *Fiona* Gordon? Charlotte glanced around the office quickly, half-expecting some female to emerge out of the shadows, but no one did. She took a breath. Maybe Fergus wasn't the father. Gordon was a clan name, after all. Lots of them around, probably. She looked up at Niall expectantly, but he appeared to be studying a painting on the wall behind the desk.

The hair at her nape prickled. Was he deliberately avoiding looking at her? He'd been very quiet on the ride over, but she'd assumed that was because Simon had accompanied them to pick up supplies while they were in town. Would Niall not have warned her that she'd be working for the father of the girl *his* father wanted him to marry? Then again, why would he? Niall didn't know Greer had told her about Fiona. And—this stung a little—maybe he wouldn't care if he did know. She was an outsider, a stray guest. Fraser family matters would have nothing to do with her.

Except, of course, they did or she wouldn't be here.

"I think ye'll find Miss MacGregor capable of clerking duties." Niall said now.

Those words brought her back to the present. Capable? Just *capable*? She found her voice. "Yes. In addition to keeping your office organized and your files up to date, I can also take notes and transcribe conversations with your clients. I can even go out and do whatever necessary research you will require."

Fergus blinked and for a moment she thought she saw something close to amusement in his gray eyes. Niall's smoke-colored gaze had darkened, though. Had she said too much? He looked more quizzical than angry, though. Probably because women didn't run around doing research these days? Women were rarely allowed to even work in business offices. She needed to remember that, if she weren't going to be asked questions she couldn't answer without sounding like someone needed to be put into an asylum.

"I have someone to do the leg-running these days," Fergus answered, "but I am quite sure he will be happy to relinquish the office routine to you. We seem to have a continuously growing stack of papers that need filing."

Filing. Vi would have a fit that someone with a master's degree in English literature would be put to filing papers. Luckily, Vi wasn't here. Charlotte knew that in the eighteenth century, filing papers in an office was considered a prestigious position. She wouldn't complain. She had, after all, wanted to *clerk*. Filing was definitely *clerical*.

She managed not to laugh at the literal irony of it.

****

Niall observed Charlotte in his peripheral vision as he pretended to focus his attention on the painting—which he'd seen dozens of times—hanging on the wall behind Fergus' desk. She'd given him a look of inquiry as though she were expecting him to explain something, but he wasn't sure what it could be, other than his own ambivalence at being at the solicitor's office in the first place. He wasn't in agreement with his father's scheme, nor was he particularly in favor of Charlotte's wanting to earn coin, although he couldn't fault her for it, either.

He wouldn't lie to himself. He didn't want Charlotte to leave. In spite of his father's and brother's suspicions—he had to admit her explanation of her arrival was a bit shaky—he still didn't think she was a spy. He admired the fact that she didn't seem to be afraid of being alone in what was basically enemy territory. His father and Simon would probably argue that proved she was a spy—how many women were that brave or independent?—but to him, those were admirable qualities. He couldn't deny that he was attracted to her, as well. Attracted. If he wanted to really be truthful with himself, he'd admit he wanted her in his bed.

Enough on that line of thinking.

"I think ye'll find Miss MacGregor capable of clerking duties," he said and then grew thoughtful at her answer. She wanted to go out and about and do "research"? He knew what his father and Simon would say to that. *Opportunity to meet with her messenger.* Luckily, Fergus cut that notion short.

"I suppose I should find Simon and leave ye here to get your bearings," he said to Charlotte and then looked at Fergus. "What time do ye want me to return?"

"Midafternoon, I think," he said. "That will give Keir time to show Miss MacGregor how things are organized and what needs to be done."

"Kier?" Charlotte asked.

"Aye. My son."

Niall thought Charlotte's face lost a bit of color, but maybe it was the lighting. "Ye remember Keir, nae? The day ye and Greer went shopping?"

"I…uh, yes…I remember." She took a breath and managed a small smile. "He seemed very nice."

To him, it didn't sound as though she meant it. He tried to remember if Keir had said anything to embarrass or upset her. His friend did push the edges of humor sometimes, but Niall didn't think he'd said anything untoward that day. There hadn't really been time for conversation. Fiona had inquired about how long she would be staying—

Fiona. Was that what Charlotte's hesitation was about? While Fiona's questions had seemed casual that day, she had not been exactly friendly. Charlotte wouldn't know why, of course, since no one had seen the kiss beneath the mistletoe, but women seemed intuitively to pick up on those kinds of things.

Niall tried to search her face, but she was looking at

Fergus, the smile—not her natural one, he saw now—still in place.

He was going to have to give this some thought, but for now, the best thing a man could do was leave.

****

Charlotte watched Niall go. For the first time since her arrival in this century, she felt truly alone. She'd been confused, certainly, and maybe a little afraid that she'd lost her mind trying to make sense of what had happened, but she'd not felt *alone*. Niall had been part of the circle dance—in which century, she wasn't quite sure—and he'd been there when she woke at his clan's castle. Since then, she'd not been out of sight of his family, other than the short time she'd spent talking with the lady at the bench of the river's bank. She hadn't realized how much she'd come to count on his presence. Somehow, she'd always felt safe. Now, she was in a law office with a stranger who might be Niall's father-in-law one day.

Mr. Gordon gestured to an armchair near the window. "If ye'd like to have a seat, Keir should be along shortly and he can show ye the proper sorting of the things on the desk."

"Thank you." She took the chair he'd indicated. "Don't you have a daughter too? I think there was someone with your son the day we ran into them."

"Aye. That would be Fiona." He smiled widely. "She's the apple of my eye, she is. Couldn't have asked my wife for a better daughter, God rest her soul."

It must have been the mother's soul that was resting, since Fiona was alive and well when they'd met. "I'm sorry if you lost your wife."

He inclined his head in acknowledgement. "A fever took her when Fiona was a wee bairn. The lass practically raised herself."

Did that mean she'd been given free rein? To run amok as she wished? She hadn't seemed meek or docile that day on the street. Quite the opposite, but perhaps Charlotte was equating Fiona's bright orange-red hair with a fiery disposition and was reading too much into an encounter that had lasted only minutes. Still. Now that Greer had told her about the circumstances, the girl's questions seemed pointed and her eyes—a pale shade of blue that looked almost silvery—had been as sharp as the metal itself when she'd looked at Charlotte.

Did she think Charlotte competition? *Was* she competition? She knew Niall was attracted to her—the kiss had proved that—but was there more? *Could* there be more? If there were, she would have to tell Niall the truth about where she was from, and that would probably quell his interest faster than a pin in a balloon. She'd be carted off to the Scottish equivalent of Bedlam. It was all so complicated.

She looked out the window to the street below, hoping to see Niall somewhere, but there were only strangers going to and fro.

She really did feel alone.

****

For once, Niall was glad Simon was with him when they went to collect Charlotte later that afternoon. They'd had to wait on a shipment coming in from Nairn, and by the time it arrived, it was already midafternoon. It would have made no sense to take the wagon home and then turn around.

Not that Niall was a coward. He didn't usually avoid conflict. In this instance, however, he was uneasy about how Charlotte's day had gone. If Fiona had shown up at the office, things might have gone awry. Niall had already witnessed her sharp inquisition that day on the street. If she harangued Charlotte with questions—especially personal ones—the lass would suspect something was amiss.

For now, he wanted to evade any discussion about Fiona. While Keir knew his sister was interested in him, he had assured Niall that his sister's attention was fleeting. Once she caught another admirer at a ceilidh, she'd refocus on her new conquest. He hoped his friend was right.

He made a quick perusal of the office when he entered and gave a thankful sigh when he didn't see Fiona. Keir and Charlotte were seated at the desk with piles of papers and engaged in congenial conversation, as far as he could tell.

Maybe too congenial? Charlotte had just laughed out loud at something Keir said that Niall couldn't hear. Damn it! Was Keir flirting with her? The man did have a natural way with women, damn it again. He took a breath. Maybe his friend was only testing Charlotte to see how she'd respond to flirtation, since Niall had told him he wanted to find out if she had any other paramours—he wouldn't say *spies*—lurking about.

"Ye look like a thunderstorm about to break." Simon raised a brow. "Did ye nae learn from Da to keep what ye are feeling from showing?"

"Of course I did," Niall all bur growled and then made an effort to appear passive. He didn't want Kier to think he was jealous. His friend would bait him no end.

Charlotte looked over, an expression of surprise on her face. "Is it time to leave already?"

Had she been having such a good time that she

didn't even know the whole day had practically passed? Niall started to furrow his brows, stopped, and attempted a smile. At least, he hoped it looked like a smile. "Aye, lass. The sun goes down early in winter."

"Did ye have a good day?" Simon actually sounded sincere.

"Yes, we did," Charlotte answered. "Keir has been very kind and terribly patient with me."

"It's been my pleasure," Keir said, "but ye are a verra quick learner." He glanced at Niall and then smiled at Charlotte. "I look forward to learning about your other talents as well."

Talents? Just what talents was Keir referring to? Niall started to glower but became aware of his brother watching him as Keir went to retrieve Charlotte's cloak and then helped her on with it.

An elbow lodged between his ribs. "Ye *did* want Keir to find out about what the lass may be up to," Simon whispered out of the corner of his mouth. "Ye'd do well to remember it."

Niall felt his teeth grind as he forced a smile to no one in particular. His brother was right, but he didn't have to like it.

Chapter Eleven

By the time Charlotte had worked for three days in Fergus Gordon's office, she felt like she had done a good amount of organizing. She'd rearranged some files for better access according to subject matter, although it seemed that the solicitor kept the personal files of his clients in his own office rather than in her area. She had also begun to feel like it was *her* desk, although she hadn't put any personal items in it or on it. Not that she actually had personal items, but a small vase of flowers might be nice. Not the season, though, nor did she want to appear territorial.

At least, Keir seemed to be satisfied with the work she'd done. He'd checked in this morning and then left, saying it looked like she could handle things. His father had seemed satisfied too, so she was beginning to breathe a bit easier.

She'd just started working on invoices that needed to be sent out when a stranger walked in. He wore the blue bonnet with its white rosette that identified him as a Jacobite, and although he wore no uniform, he had the regal bearing of a commander. His voice, while low and well-modulated, held authority.

"Is Fergus in? 'Tis important," he said.

"May I say who's calling?" she asked.

"David Alcho."

Charlotte got up, knocked on Mr. Gordon's door,

then poked her head inside. "There is a Mr. Alcho here to see you."

Fergus stood up. "That's *Lord* Alcho, son of the Earl of Wemyss." His tone sounded like she should have known. "Show him in at once."

She did as he instructed, feeling a bit chastised. How was she to know the man was an earl's son? She'd almost forgotten that Scots did have peerage titles just like the English, and he hadn't called himself a lord. She was about to close the door when she heard him speak.

"Major General Huske is marching this way from Edinburgh."

'Ye've checked your source?" Fergus asked.

The other man chuckled. "I am the source. General Murray left me in charge at Linlithgow. My scouts reported roughly four thousand men."

"About half the English army in these parts," Fergus said.

"Aye. I suspect General Hawley will be bringing the rest in another contingent."

"Ye are most likely right," Fergus replied. "Do ye want me to send word to the prince at Bannockburn?"

"I've already done that, as well as alerting Murray and Drummond, since the duke is heading up the second regiment at Stirling. They need to be prepared for what's coming."

'Yes and…" The solictor's voice trailed off.

Charlotte heard his footsteps approaching the door and hastily took her seat at the desk. A moment later she heard the door click closed. She was trembling, whether from fear at almost being caught eavesdropping or the actuality of hearing about generals and dukes and battle strategies. This was real. She remembered something about the battle at Falkirk being only a partial victory.

Would the Frasers be called on to fight? So far, Simon's father had managed to keep most of his clan at home, although there were regular daily routines the men practiced. She didn't want Niall going off to battle. Was there anything she could do to stop him? She felt she had an obligation to tell him what she'd heard, but she didn't want that knowledge to encourage him to go.

She was still in a quandary when the front door to the office opened again. This time it was no soldier or aristocrat, but Charlotte's breath caught anyway. The one person she had hoped she wouldn't have to see, but apparently this was not going to be a good day.

Fiona Gordon walked into the room.

Before either of them had a chance to say anything, Fergus' door opened and he and his guest stepped out. Mr.—*Lord*—Alcho smiled widely when he saw Fiona.

"Miss Gordon. How very nice to see you again."

Fiona dimpled. "'Tis my pleasure to see ye, my lord."

"I wish I had time to visit with ye today," Alcho said, "but business calls."

"Och, the Cause," Fiona said. "I will be glad when the prince finally puts King George in his place and we can go back to having fun again."

"That is my wish as well," Alcho replied. "I miss the ceilidhs and sharing a dance with ye."

"Hopefully, soon. Soon." Fergus said. "Mayhap this will all be over."

Charlotte wished it would as well, but not for the reasons they'd just given. Right now, she didn't care about parties and dances. Culloden wouldn't take place if the English were defeated at Falkirk.

"So what brings ye to my office?" Fergus asked his daughter after Alcho left. "Ye doona come verra often."

"Keir mentioned your new clerk was the one I met earlier. The one who was visiting the Frasers." She glanced at Charlotte. "I didna expect ye'd be staying long enough to seek employment."

Although Fiona's tone was pleasant enough, Charlotte knew the words were code for *Why are you still here?* Or more likely, if the steely glint in the other girl's eyes was any clue, *When are you leaving?* She thought quickly. "I won't be able to return home for a bit, so I thought I'd make myself useful."

That was true since she had no idea of how—or if—she'd return to her own century. Strangely, that thought no longer produced the panic it originally had, but that was because of her emerging feelings toward Niall. Feelings she should be repressing, from what Greer had told her. She would have to be careful not to display those thoughts, not with anyone—but especially not with Fiona.

Fergus nodded. "Miss MacGregor has been quite helpful these past days."

"So Keir has said." Fiona smiled brightly although the smile didn't reach her eyes. "I decided I need to get to know this talented lady better. I thought we might go to lunch."

"Excellent idea!" Her father all but beamed at her. "That is very kind of ye, daughter."

"'Tis the least I can do," she answered, "since it seems she is quite alone in these parts."

Charlotte wanted to say that she was sitting right there, but she really wouldn't have minded if the floor had opened up and let her disappear. The last thing she wanted to do was go to lunch with Fiona. It would be an inquisition, and she didn't have answers for lots of questions. She would also have to tread carefully on being quizzed about Niall, which she was sure was Fiona's real purpose.

Then again, maybe she could find out some answers of her own.

****

"So where is home?" Fiona asked, once they were seated in the dining area of an inn a few blocks away.

Remembering that she was using the name MacGregor and not Campbell, Charlotte thought quickly. Since the MacGregors were proscribed they had lost many of their holdings and, given the bounty the English were offering, they were known as Children of the Mist since they would quickly disappear into it. Where was it misty a lot of the time? She wished Thea were here, because her friend was spot-on with geography. Then she remembered an area she had visited once before. The Trossachs.

With the combinations of several lochs and high monros, low-lying fog and mist covered much of the area. Still, better not to be too specific, especially since she was making this up. "Near Loch Lomond." She sighed slightly. "But I'm afraid we no longer have an actual home, thanks to the English."

Fiona gave her a steady look. "In that case, I would think ye'd be happy to be betrothed to the man ye are running away from."

Charlotte started. "Where did you hear that?"

"I overheard Niall telling my brother."

What else had Niall shared? Or when? Not that it probably mattered. People were bound to inquire about a "guest" who seemed to be a permanent resident at the Frasers. She might have to do some more thinking about her alibi, though. One of the reasons she always outlined the plots for her novels was because it was too easy to trip up on the details if she didn't. This time, she wasn't writing a novel. She was plotting the imaginary history about her life. If she were caught in a lie, she'd be booted out of Castle Dounie by either Niall's father or Simon and maybe even by Niall himself. She suspected he wouldn't forgive being deceived.

Fiona widened her eyes. "Is it nae true?"

She must have been quiet for too long. "Yes… it's true." She shrugged. "I just do not like talking about it."

"What was wrong with him?"

Most people would have let the matter drop, but obviously Fiona wasn't one of them. "He… We just did not suit."

"Why nae?"

Charlotte suppressed her favorite cuss word. The girl wasn't going to give up. She thought about her cousin Colin Grant, currently living innocently in Texas. Maybe she could describe him. "The man is older than me and has been married before." Not a lie. Colon *was* two years older and *had* been married briefly to a woman he'd met online. It hadn't worked out.

Fiona's eyes narrowed speculatively. "Ye are looking for a younger man who's single?"

Oh-oh. Charlotte knew where *that* question was going. No way was she going to admit being attracted to Niall. "I am not looking for anyone."

"Nae?"

"Nae. I mean, no. I…have no wish to marry." That was more or less true as well. It wasn't that she didn't want to marry. She'd just not met a man—in the twenty-first century—who created more than a spark of interest. That spark usually burned itself out after a few dates for one reason or another.

Fiona's eyebrows rose. "Never?"

Would she never drop this subject? Charlotte looked around for the waiter, hoping their food would come, but no such luck. She turned back to Fiona. "I don't much like being told what to do, and it seems to me that once a woman marries, she is subject to her husband's whims. I like my independence." Okay, maybe she was on a roll here and could change the subject. "That's why I wanted to work in your father's law office. I can earn my own money, which allows me to make my own decisions."

"I canna fault ye for that." Fiona still looked skeptical, though. "How long do ye plan to stay at Castle Dounie before ye move on, then?"

She *really* wouldn't let the matter drop, would she? "I don't know. Lord Fraser has extended an invitation to stay as long as I need to."

Fiona leveled a look on her that could have pinned her to the wall if she'd been sitting near one. The girl leaned forward.

"Since that is the case, let me be clear. My father expects Niall and me to be betrothed verra soon." She leaned back. "Niall Fraser is mine."

Charlotte smiled weakly, thankful that the waiter finally arrived with the food and sparing her an answer. A few minutes ago she'd been looking forward to digging into the steaming beef pie with its delicious aromas, but she had lost her appetite now.

What Greer had told her must have been true, then. A betrothal was in the works for Niall and Fiona.

So she had gotten her answer. It just wasn't the one she'd hoped for.

Chapter Twelve

"Ye are awfully quiet," Niall said on the way home that afternoon. "Was there a problem at the office?"

Yes. Fiona Gordon showed up. Of course, Charlotte couldn't tell Niall that, or at least, not the reason *why* the girl had come to the office. Nor could she confront Niall about the situation, especially since Greer had, more or less, confirmed the story. Apart from *that* small fact, Charlotte had no dibs on the man, particularly since she hadn't exposed the much bigger fact that she was from the future. She sighed.

Niall gave her a worried look. "Ye doona have to earn coin if ye are nae happy with the work."

"It isn't that." She tried to shake off her bad mood. This was one of the few afternoons that Niall actually came to collect her by himself. Usually either Simon was with him or one of the groomsmen was sent. Under normal circumstances, she would be deliriously happy with being alone with Niall, even for the short ride home in the buggy. Niall was watching her, though, so she needed to say something.

"I am somewhat worried about what I overheard at the office today." That was true at least.

He raised a brow. "Which was?"

"A Mister, er—*Lord*—David Alcho came in—"

"Colonel Alcho was here?"

So the man was a colonel in addition to being a lord.

"Um, Mr. Gordon only said he was the son of an earl—"

"Same person. What did he say?"

She should have guessed the man was a soldier with high rank, given his bearing and the conversation she'd heard. "He said a General Huske was marching from Edinburgh with four thousand men."

"Not good." Niall's face darkened. "He's second-in-command up here."

"Is General Hawley the first in command?"

"Aye." He knotted his brows. "What did ye hear about him, lass?"

She hated imparting more bad news. "That Hawley is probably following him."

She hesitated, then added. "They're heading for Stirling, I think."

Niall nodded. "That would make sense since we've laid siege to the castle."

"But they're going to fight at Falkirk."

His attention snapped to her. "Falkirk? That's only halfway to Stirling. Did Alcho say General Murray was going to lie in wait for them there?"

For a moment, her blood turned to ice as she realized she'd made a blunder. There had been no talk about Jacobites diverting to Falkirk. The reason she knew it was because she'd read it in the history books. In the twenty-first century. The English army would stop in Falkirk for the night and the Jacobites would attack, having been warned of the approaching soldiers. She took a deep breath. So…maybe it didn't matter that *that* conversation had not actually taken place this afternoon. It was going to happen anyway. "That seemed to be the plan."

Niall considered, then nodded. "'Tis probably a good one. Huske will nae be expecting either Murray or Drummond's men to leave the siege, so they will have the element of surprise." A corner of his mouth lifted. "'Twould be better to confront only four thousand men than the whole army."

He saw humor in that? Charlotte would never understand why men saw war as a game, of sorts. "I hope no one is killed."

That took the half-smile off his face. "Och, lass. 'Tis what happens."

"But it doesn't have to."

His brows knitted. "What do ye mean?"

She was probably venturing into boggy land, but if she had been sent here to keep Culloden from happening, this was as good a time as any to start. "Would it be possible for one of the Scottish generals to meet with the English one to negotiate?"

He blinked and Charlotte tried not to wince. No doubt he thought she was daft. Or, more likely, that she shouldn't be offering an opinion at all since women weren't supposed to have any. She lifted her chin. "I suppose you think I am being silly."

"Nae. I think ye are a smart lass. 'Twould be a wonderful solution." He shook his head. "'Tis just nae possible."

She felt a little guilty about thinking Niall might be a chauvinist. She shouldn't have assumed it since he'd never acted like one. "Why isn't it, then?"

"The Scots have been fighting this war ever since James the Second and Seventh was deposed. His son, Prince Charlie's father, tried to regain the throne in 1708. This is nae the first uprising." He grew quiet as he guided the horses across the bridge into the bailey. "I hope this one will be the last."

Charlotte bit her tongue. It was going to be the last, but not in the way he hoped.

****

"I doona ken why we are doing this," Niall said that evening as he walked with his father and Simon to the front steps of Fergus' home in Inverness. "He sent us word that Colonel Alcho had stopped in to tell him about the English advancing. He didna request a conference about it."

"I want all the details," his father answered and let the brass knocker fall.

"'Tis nothing we can do to help, being over a hundred miles away," Niall muttered as the door opened.

Neither his father nor Simon answered him, although Simon gave him a sideways look as they were ushered into the parlor.

Fergus joined them a few minutes later, along with Fiona. Niall looked around for Keir, then remembered he'd gone to Nairn earlier and probably hadn't gotten back yet.

Fergus poured each of them a dram of whisky—sherry for Fiona—and then settled in his armchair by the fire, gesturing Simon and his father to take the other two armchairs, which left Niall to share the sofa with Fiona. From her self-satisfied smile, he wondered if she'd asked her father to manipulate the seating arrangement. When she moved closer to him, he was almost sure of it. He didn't miss the benevolent looks both her father and his gave them, either.

"I am so glad ye chose to visit tonight," she said. "'Tis been a while since Yule."

It had been not quite three weeks. Why was she mentioning Yule anyway? Was she still thinking about that kiss under the mistletoe? In hindsight, it had been a pretty stupid thing for him to do, but he honestly didn't think Fiona would hold strong memories of it.

"We've been busy conditioning the men so they'll be ready when the call comes to fight," he replied.

"Which brings us to why we're here tonight," Simon said. "Your father sent word that Colonel Alcho visited today."

Niall wasn't sure if Simon was just impatient to get to the point or if his brother recognized there was an undercurrent between Fiona and himself. Either way, he was thankful the conversation had been diverted.

'Aye," his father said. "What's this business of Murray's plan to attack Huske at Falkirk?"

Fergus looked puzzled. "Falkirk? Alcho didna mention a battle there."

His father glanced at him, then turned back to Fergus. "Ye are sure?"

"Aye. All he said was the Duke of Perth—that'd be Drummond, not Murray—was marching to Stirling via Falkirk," Fergus replied. "Why do ye think that?"

His father and Simon both turned to him. Niall regretted now having told them what Charlotte had said. It seemed the thing to do after Fergus had sent word about the English on the march toward Stirling. He'd just assumed that the solicitor hadn't wanted to put too much information into a written message.

He certainly didn't want to make matters worse by letting Fergus know that Charlotte had overheard his conversation. He might very well let her go if he thought she was eavesdropping. Charlotte would then want to find another job and there weren't many opportunities in Inverness that didn't leave a lass vulnerable. Niall had already recognized a stubborn streak in her and, truthfully, he couldn't fault her for wanting to earn some coin. He wouldn't want to be totally dependent on hosts who were no relation. However, he avoided looking at his brother and father when he answered.

"I must have reached that conclusion after remembering that Murray had split the Jacobite forces in two and that one of them—Drummond, not Murray—would be coming to Stirling via Falkirk." He managed a shrug. "Too much strategizing on my part."

"I suppose it could be something they might consider," Fergus replied after some thought.

Fergus seemed to accept the theory, although Simon and his father looked skeptical. At least, neither one of them said anything. He'd probably be barraged by questions from both of them later.

For now, though, he had a question himself. Where had Charlotte come up with that idea?

****

Charlotte had been half-expecting the summons ever since a rider showed up yesterday with the news that the English general had been routed at Falkirk, so she wasn't surprised when it came.

What did surprise her, though, was that Niall was alone in the study when she arrived. He was seated behind the desk instead of in one of the armchairs by the hearth, and he wasn't smiling. Neither of those things bode well, but she'd been expecting his father and brother to be in attendance too. She said a brief prayer of thanks that they weren't there.

"Sit." He pointed to the straight-back chair in front

of the desk and then added, “Please.”

She sat, folded her hands in her lap, and stayed quiet. He leaned back and studied her. The silence grew nearly deafening. She willed herself not to squirm and forced herself to meet his gaze.

Finally, he reached for a paper. “Ye are aware we were sent this missive yesterday?”

“Yes.”

“Do ye want to read it?”

“No.”

He gave her another steady look before he glanced down at it. “Allow me to rekindle my memory, then.”

She doubted very much that he hadn’t memorized every word, but she said nothing.

“It says here,” he tapped the paper, “that General Drummond turned south to distract the English scouts. Meanwhile, General Murray joined up with MacDonalds and turned back to Falkirk. They arrived late in the afternoon with dusk approaching. Huske’s left flank was destroyed.” He laid the paper down and looked at Charlotte.

“That’s good, isn’t it?” she managed to say.

“Aye, but probably a matter of luck. ’Twas raining and the field was muddy. The dragoons’ horses churning the ground up made it hard for the infantry to follow. Murray’s men were to their right and a bog to their left, so they didna have much choice.”

“But the Scots won.”

“Not entirely. Huske’s right flank held firm. Because of the weather conditions and falling darkness, the Scots didna press on. By morning, Huske’s men had escaped back to Edinburgh.”

Charlotte tried to read Niall’s expression, but could

tell nothing. "Isn't retreating a good thing?"

"Aye." He stared hard at her for what seemed like half an eternity. "Did ye send word to warn Huske?"

"*What*?" Charlotte had not been expecting that accusation. "No. Of course not. *No*. Why would I?"

He sighed. "Doona make this harder for both of us than it already is."

"I don't understand."

"I asked Da to let me talk to ye first." He gave her another intent look. "Neither Da nor Simon believes the story ye told about how ye arrived here. Ye had nae chaperone, nor clothing nor coin—"

"I explained all that. I was running away from a betrothal I didn't want."

Niall didn't answer right away. Instead, he opened a drawer and pulled out another letter and laid it on the desk. "Ye may want to read this one. It came yesterday too."

She eyed it warily. She hadn't noticed another messenger yesterday, but there had been men coming and going. She picked it up carefully as though it might suddenly develop life and attack her. When she saw the letterhead—from Fort William—dread filled her. After she finished reading the short message, her blood chilled. She put the letter down.

"There is no Colin Grant at Fort William." Niall's voice was calm. "There is no betrothal, is there?"

"I…" She couldn't think of a thing to say. She didn't want to come up with another lie. "No."

"I asked Da to let me speak to ye first because he can be… Well, let's just say I wanted to spare ye that."

"Thank you." She meant that sincerely.

"Da and Simon think ye are a spy." His voice was

flat. "I didna want to believe it—I doona want to believe it."

"I am no spy. I swear it."

He gave her a level look. "Then how did ye ken the Scots would attack at Falkirk?"

"I told you I overheard the conversation in Mr. Gordon's office."

"A conversation in which an attack on Falkirk was never mentioned. Da questioned Fergus about it." He sighed again. "Ye have to be honest with me, lass."

Honest. Dear Lord. How honest could she be? She couldn't fault Niall—or even his father or brother—for doubting her story. It had holes enough in it to make a fine sieve. However, being arrested for being a traitor was another matter. She was pretty sure there was a Scottish equivalent to being imprisoned in the Tower of London. But the truth? She looked at Niall, only to find him watching her passively. Could she tell him? Did she have a choice? She took a deep breath.

"The reason I knew what was going to happen at Falkirk was because I read it in a history book."

His expression changed to confusion. "A history book? How could ye do that when it hadn't happened?"

She squared her shoulders. "Because I am from the future."

Chapter Thirteen

If there was one response Niall hadn't anticipated, that was it. Charlotte was from the future? He wasn't sure if that statement was better than the other lies she'd been telling.

"Ye canna expect me to believe that." He sighed. "I ken, now, that ye made up the story about a betrothed. I need the truth. Are ye a spy?"

"No."

"Then why would ye lie to us?"

Charlotte gave him a look that he couldn't decipher. "Because you would not believe the truth."

He strove to keep his voice modulated when he spoke. "'Tis impossible. Ye canna go around saying such a thing. Ye'll be carted away."

"Which is why I didn't tell you."

There was no guile in Charlotte's tone or expression. She sounded as though she sincerely believed what she said. He paused. What if…? "Have ye escaped from an asylum, lass? Is that what ye were trying to hide by claiming a betrothed?"

"No, I—"

"'Twould make sense," Niall went on. "'Twould explain why ye had nae clothes or coin or chaperone."

"I am not insane. You have to believe that much," Charlotte said.

He blinked. "I doona think ye are insane, lass. 'Tis

a sad fact that, too often, if a woman poses problems for her husband or kin, she is locked away in an attic or a physician declares her nae fit and she disappears into a madhouse, nae to be seen again."

"I haven't posed any problems…" She stopped and chewed her lip, a trait Niall found intriguing in spite of the conversation they were having. "Please believe me."

He wanted to. Not the part of being from the future, but that she had escaped some form of imprisonment. By now, he'd seen enough of her independent spirit and tenacity to doubt any man could bend her to his will. And there were men who got angered by that.

"Ye will be safe here. Ye have my word." He nodded for emphasis. "Even if I could, I would not send ye back to wherever ye came from."

A strange sound came from Charlotte's throat. At first, he thought she was choking, for her face had turned red, her eyes were tightly shut, and she bent forward, clutching her stomach. Just as he started to rise to help her, another strange sound occurred. This one grew louder until he recognized it as laughter. He watched warily as the wild, nearly hysterical laughter grew louder, as if she could not contain herself.

For the first time, he wondered if perhaps he'd been wrong and there was something truly wrong with Charlotte.

****

She couldn't stop laughing. She *should* stop. She *needed* to stop. She knew she was doing herself no favors by acting this way, but she couldn't stop. The irony of what Niall had said—even though he had no idea—was just too *ironic*. As if he could just say something in Gaelic and wave a sword or something and—*poof!*—

she'd be back in Texas checking her email. The idea was just too…*funny*. She laughed harder, hearing a strange wailing sound coming from somewhere and realized she was the one producing it. Then she felt strong hands wrap around her arms and lift her, shaking her gently.

She hiccupped, then sputtered as tears started falling.

She became aware that Niall was holding her, rubbing her back in soothing circles as he *did* mutter something in Gaelic, although the words didn't transport her anywhere. She breathed in the warm scent of him, mixed with leather and soap, and felt a calm wash over her. She wanted to cling to him forever. Slowly, she disengaged and looked up.

He watched her with a guarded expression. Not that she could blame him. He probably thought she was more than a bit daft. She'd been acting unhinged.

"I'm… sorry," she said as she hiccupped again. "I just…what you said about sending me back…it was just too much."

His brow furrowed. "What do ye mean?"

Should she tell him about the irony? She felt more stable now, the threat of another hysterical episode under control. He probably wouldn't believe her. *She* wouldn't believe herself either if she weren't currently experiencing the eighteenth century instead of the twenty-first.

The easiest thing for her to do would be to let him think she had escaped from some sort of asylum and that she feared being institutionalized. *That* would certainly be true. He had promised she'd be safe here. She could stay and no one would know she'd time-travelled. She could still try to keep the battle at Culloden from happening.

But she was tired of lying. She took a deep breath.

"I ask for your patience and tolerance for what I am about to say."

He nodded, his eyes not leaving her face. "Go ahead."

"I appreciate that you are allowing me to stay here. I think, for the present, the idea that I have escaped from being imprisoned unfairly is a sound one, especially if it will eliminate suspicion that I am an English spy." She stopped and took a deep breath. "But it is not true. I *am* from the future."

His expression turned troubled. "Ye need to stop saying that lest someone—like my da—hears ye."

"I understand. Your father would think me mad. But I want you to know." She hesitated again. "The Jacobites are going to give up the siege on Stirling and make their way to Inverness very soon."

Niall's eyes widened. "How do ye ken that?"

She gave him a faint smile. "I already told you how I know."

"But…" He frowned. "Why would the prince's men retreat to the north when it would be more advantageous to hold the borderlands?"

"I do not know the strategy behind it," Charlotte said. "I only know that they will come." She didn't add what the final outcome would be. This was not the time. "If what I told you comes to pass, will you believe me?"

He closed his eyes and didn't answer immediately. Charlotte waited, since there was nothing more she could say. Finally, he opened them and looked at her.

"I just might," he said.

****

Niall looked at his family members gathered around the table in the council room. He'd asked them to meet with him after dinner so he could share the conversation he'd had with Charlotte. Not all of it. Just the version they'd agreed would be best for now.

"So," he said as he finished, "I think we can agree that Charlotte is not a spy."

Greer nodded even though his father and brother looked skeptical. "Everything she has told us makes sense if she escaped some kind of involuntary confinement. It would even make sense that she wore MacGregor tartan. Her family—or whoever kept her prisoner—wouldn't suspect she'd identify with a clan that's proscribed."

"That's a risk in itself, though," Simon said dryly. "She could be *legally* arrested and confined."

Greer waved a hand. "Maybe along the Borders where the lowlanders want to let the English think they're loyal, but this far north, a MacGregor would be safe, especially a woman."

"True enough," Niall said. "Frasers have nae quarrel with MacGregors."

"Which is probably why she chose to make her way here," Greer said. "'Twas clever of her."

Niall certainly wouldn't argue the point that Charlotte was clever. She had discerned—somehow—that Murray's men were going to attack at Falkirk. He still wasn't quite sure what to make of her claim to be from the future. Mayhap she'd had a head injury before Hogmanay that she didn't remember. That might account for such a strange tale. Or maybe she *had* been confined somewhere and still didn't trust him enough to tell him where, for fear of being sent back. That thought stung a bit.

He hated having to deceive Greer, but having his father and brother believe the story he'd given them would keep Charlotte safe for now, until he could think things through to a logical conclusion.

"Clever enough," Simon agreed, but still looked unconvinced. "I wonder if her real name is even Campbell."

His father looked at him sharply. "Why do ye say that?"

Simon raised a brow. "'Tis just a thought, since she hasna exactly been truthful with us on other things."

Niall felt his temper stir. "It would hardly be *clever* of her to call herself a Campbell at Inverness, would it? 'Tis nae love lost between us and the colonel at the fort."

"True." Greer frowned at her brother. "Why can ye nae accept who she is?"

"Because I doona ken who she is," Simon answered.

"Never mind that for now." Their father turned to Niall. "I am more interested in finding out how she knew about the attack at Falkirk when Fergus said Alcho hadn't mentioned it."

So his father had not believed him. Or, mayhap, he wanted Niall to tell him again. His father wasn't referred to as "the Fox" for nothing. One of his favorite strategies was getting people to repeat themselves to see if he could catch them in a lie.

"I already told ye that it was assumption on my part." He shrugged. "She may have agreed with me."

"It doesna matter now, does it?" Greer asked. "So can we drop the matter? Charlotte has done nae harm and has only been helpful. The two of ye are always suspicious of everything."

Neither his brother or father answered, but Niall didn't think that meant they agreed with her. He could practically hear their minds churning.

Not that his own wasn't churning too. There were still too many questions left unanswered, including the most important one.

Who really was Charlotte Campbell? He had to admit he had no idea.

Chapter Fourteen

"Ye seem restless today," Greer remarked as she moved a chess piece on the board that had been set up in the solar.

Charlotte glanced out the window where swirling snow blocked any view and the low gray clouds let hardly any light in through the window where the sun usually shone through in the afternoons. "I just don't like being stuck inside all day."

As soon as the words were out, she regretted saying them. Greer gave her a quick cursory glance before intensely studying the chessboard as though one of the pieces might have moved itself. The whole family had been watching her since she'd made the new claim a few days ago that she had escaped from involuntary confinement elsewhere. They weren't overt about it. Most of the glances were sidelong or suddenly focused on something near her if she looked at them, but Charlotte could feel the general uneasiness. Were they waiting for her to have some sort of episode? Or maybe go on a lunatic rant? She couldn't really blame them for being cautious. She had not gone into detail—there weren't any details—about why she had been confined or for what. She supposed she should consider herself lucky that they still allowed her a knife at the dinner table. She really needed to clarify.

"I meant that I don't like stormy weather."

"Aye." Greer looked up, her expression neutral. "Hopefully the blizzard will nae last long this time."

"I hope not. I hate to think of anyone being out in this."

Greer smiled. "Ye mean Niall?"

Charlotte felt her face warm. Niall had left yesterday morning before the storm broke, headed for Dingwall to check the capacity of the harbor to accept French military vessels.

She wanted to tell him that the French would not be sending any more reinforcements to aid Scotland, but it was a fact she could not prove. He was still not convinced that what she'd told him was true. She didn't want him doubting her further. Right now, though, she was more worried about his safety.

"I just hope he didn't get caught out in the storm."

"Doona fash. He's been out in worse."

"Worse?"

"Aye. This far north, squalls coming off the Moray Firth turn into blizzards quickly. He probably stayed at Dingwall."

"But if he didn't? If he's out in this—" Charlotte let her voice trail off. She'd probably already expressed too much interest if the amused look on Greer's face was any indication. She needed to be cautious in showing concern, since not only had Fiona made quite clear her intentions regarding Niall—which no doubt her father would approve—but Greer herself had told her about *their* father's expectations.

"There are abandoned crofter's cottages around, as well as shepherd sheds. He'll find cover." Greer studied her. "Do ye care for him, then?"

"No! I mean…well, yes, of course, I care." Dear

Lord, she was making a mess of this. "I mean…I don't him to freeze to death out there."

Greer scrutinized her a moment longer. "He'll be safe." She said it quietly and pointed to the board. "'Tis your turn to move."

Was it her move? She wasn't thinking about chess. She was wondering what she should do next to convince Niall that she spoke true. Looking at Greer, Charlotte wasn't sure that Greer accepted her explanation, but at least she wasn't going to pursue an interrogation. She looked at the board and moved a knight to block the previous move. It was slightly ironic since "knight" might have been a fitting description of Niall if they'd been in the Middle Ages. She quickly dismissed that fantasy.

It wouldn't do to let anyone think she was interested in him. That was a sure way to lose her job and get boosted out of Castle Dounie at the same time. And then what would she do? Where would she go?

Much better to keep her feelings to herself, even though she suspected she was falling in love with him.

Better he didn't know that either.

****

"Rub him down well and give him a hot mash," Niall told the stable boy as he turned his horse over along with a coin for the lad.

"Aye, sir! Thank ye!" The boy pocketed the shilling more quickly than a sleight-of-hand performer at a local fair. Niall managed to hide a laugh, knowing his horse would be well looked after.

"I'll come see to him in the morning, then."

"Aye, sir!" the boy said again. "I'll take special care of him."

Niall made his way to a nearby inn. They'd been only a few miles away from Dingwall when the storm hit. He'd considered continuing on but decided against it. January storms could be brutal, especially when they sprang up as suddenly as this one had. Better to wait for it to blow over.

But that meant it would be another day or two—or possibly more, depending on when the storm would pass—before he got home. He didn't like leaving Charlotte to fend for herself that long, knowing both Simon and his father still had doubts about her. His father's questioning methods could be subtle when he chose, and Charlotte might easily get tangled in her own words. A *third* version of how she got to Inverness—especially claiming she was from the future—would end his father's tolerance. He'd most likely turn her over to one of the generals for real interrogation. That wouldn't even be the worst of it. With the Redcoats amassing in Edinburgh, both Murray and Drummond would be focused on blocking them. They wouldn't be paying much attention to a lone woman prisoner who would be at the mercy of guards who weren't even trained soldiers.

Niall hoped he could count on Greer, even though he wasn't sure his sister totally believed Charlotte either, but she had offered to stay close to her while he was gone.

He would have preferred to bring Charlotte with him. It would have given him a chance to question her about what else the "history books" had said about this war. Maybe she could tell him when to expect the reinforcement of French troops… He stopped himself. Did he really think she knew the future? Or was he driving himself to madness? He shook his head. In any case, propriety prevented him from even suggesting that she accompany him.

"Ye are a lucky man," the innkeeper told him when he inquired about a room. "We've got just one left."

"I guess a lot of travelers decided nae to take a chance out there."

"On a night like this, 'twould be madness to venture out."

And yet Niall had almost done that. Even now he was questioning whether he should be leaving Charlotte at the mercy of his father. Perhaps he was descending into a madness all his own that had nothing to do with the storm.

"It's a good thing ye've got a room left, then."

"Aye. 'Twas another gent in here earlier. He said he'd be back, but since he's nae here now…" The innkeeper looked at him expectantly.

Niall repressed a sigh. What the man was saying was that it was going to cost him more. Instead of bartering—he wasn't in the mood—he simply pulled out more than enough coin. "Will this do?"

"Aye." The man snatched the money almost as quickly as the stable boy had, but this time Niall didn't feel like laughing. "Which way to the room?"

"Down the hall. Last on the left."

Niall half-expected the room to be shabby and cold, but he was pleasantly surprised to find a small fire burning in the brazier and an oil lamp on the nearby table. Lighting the lamp, he looked around. The wallpaper wasn't peeling, the upholstery on the armchair near the brazier wasn't worn, and the bed had a clean quilt neatly tucked in. At least the money he'd spent was worth it.

He eyed the bed again. It looked comfortable and was large enough for two. His thoughts turned to Charlotte once more and visualized the two of them tucked under that quilt together, limbs entangled, basking in the afterglow of— *Enough*. There was no sense in torturing himself.

But he had a hard time falling asleep that night, and images of a naked Charlotte filled his dreams when he did.

****

Niall looked around the table as he entered the small room off the kitchens where the family sometimes broke their fast when their presence was not needed in the Great Hall. He'd gotten home late last night after having to wait out the blizzard for three days, and he hadn't had a real conversation with anyone.

From all appearances, things seemed to be normal. Engaged in conversation with Greer, Charlotte looked unscathed. Neither his father nor Simon were paying attention to them, which made him breathe a sigh of relief as he sat down.

The relief was short-lived.

"Did ye hear the news up at Dingwall?" Simon asked.

The hairs at his nape prickled. "News?"

"Aye. The Jacobites left the siege at Stirling."

Those hairs now rose. He glanced sideways at Charlotte, but she was studiously stirring sugar into her porridge. Was this what she had meant? Or was it coincidental? He looked at Simon. "Why?"

His brother shrugged. "It seems not everyone was in agreement about who the victor was at Falkirk."

Niall frowned. "Shouldn't that be clear? Hawley

retreated to Edinburgh."

"He did, eventually. We got a missive while you were gone. It seems some of Murray's and Drummond's men didn't realize that Hawley's left flank had been routed while the right flank held firm, and they fled the battle."

"Cowards," his father said.

Ignoring his father's outburst, Niall asked, "How many?"

"Several hundred, maybe more," Simon answered. "The letter wasn't specific on that detail, but it seems to have put Murray and Drummond at odds about whose fault it was about the confusion."

"Understandable, I suppose," Niall said, "given that they had split the army in two before Falkirk. Even if the generals had conferred, word may not have reached the rank and file, considering they were on opposite sides of the battle."

"True enough, but the prince is nae happy," Simon replied, "especially with Murray."

Their father snorted. "'Tis because the prince doesna want to take the advice of a seasoned man who kens what he's doing."

"'Tis a good thing the door is closed, Da." Although most Highlanders wanted to remove the Hanoverian king from the throne and return a Stuart, not all of them had that much confidence in the prince, although no one spoke it aloud. The prince was young, hot-headed, inclined to imbibe in too much whisky, and had grown up in Italy and France.

"Aye." Simon looked at Charlotte and then back to Niall. "Since we doona ken the facts, 'tis better we nae discuss it."

In front of Charlotte. Niall could almost hear the unspoken words, which meant his brother—and most likely his father—still suspected she might be a spy. He was tempted to point out that if she *were* a spy, ironically what his father had said would be welcome news in an English camp. He held his peace, though, and Simon's next words made him glad he had.

"The army is coming to Inverness to reorganize."

Niall felt his blood chill. This time, when he looked at Charlotte, she met his gaze calmly. He felt numb. What she had predicted was coming true. She had *known.*

Chapter Fifteen

"You have questions, I presume?" Charlotte asked Niall. They were back in the study—she hadn't needed a summons—but this time, they were seated in the armchairs near the hearth where a fire blazed cheerfully as if there were no concerns to be had.

He shook his head. "Just one. *How*?"

She didn't bother asking him to clarify what he meant. "I don't know how I got here."

"Ye doona ken?"

Her turn to shake her head. "All I know is that one minute I was dancing in the Hogmanay circle at Inverness. You were there—"

"I ken that, lass."

She paused, scrutinizing his face. He wasn't going to like what she said next. "It wasn't in this century."

His eyes widened, then narrowed. "'Tis impossible."

"It happened." She hesitated again. "You asked me for a kiss after the dance—"

"Nae! *That* I would remember." In spite of the direction of the conversation, he managed a quirky grin. "Believe me."

She felt her face warm as memory flooded through her. Better move on for now, though. "The last thing I remember is that kiss. Then I woke up here at Castle Dounie."

He stared at her for a long moment. “What I remember is dancing with ye and introducing ourselves afterward. Ye couldna find your friends and I think ye panicked, because ye swooned.” He took a deep breath. “There was nae a kiss.”

She pursed her lips. “In *my* century there was.”

He studied her again. “What century was that?”

Now it was her turn to take a deep breath. “The twenty-first.”

“The twenty-first.”

His voice was flat, his expression neutral. He sat perfectly still and Charlotte wondered if he even considered believing her. More likely, he thought her completely mad and that she might suddenly become violent if he moved. She forced herself to remain still as well.

Finally, he spoke. “’Twould be three hundred years from now.”

“Not quite.” She took another deep breath. “I know this makes no sense, but I swear it is what happened. The reason I knew the Jacobites would return to Inverness is because I read it in a history book.” She searched her memory for what the army was going to do next and, thankfully, remembered. “Their next goal will be to take Fort George.”

Niall frowned. “That would be logical since it is near here in Inverness. Ye wouldna need a history book to figure that out.”

“Perhaps not.” She thought harder. “I think I also read that General Hawley will be replaced by the Duke of Cumberland.”

He started. “Cumberland? He’s in London with his brother, the king.”

"He was." She tried to make her voice sound confident. "He's on his way to Edinburgh and should arrive by the end of the month."

Niall sat quietly for so long after that statement that Charlotte wondered if she'd put him into a catatonic state on the brink of madness himself. Finally, he seemed to revive. "If what ye say comes to pass, ye either have direct contact with King George—"

"I do not. I will swear that by anything you want me to."

"Or…" he hesitated once more. "I will have to believe ye."

"Fair enough. I didn't expect you to just accept something that *seems* impossible. It seems impossible to me too." She rose. "May I leave now?"

"Aye. I've much to think over."

She'd only gotten as far as the doorway when he called on her to wait. She turned. "Yes?"

"I have one question."

"What is it?"

"Will the Scots win this war?"

She felt tears suddenly well up in her eyes. "No, you will not."

And then she turned and ran.

****

Niall wanted to jump up and run after her, but her terse reply had left him nonplussed. What had possessed him to even ask that question? Did he really think she was from the future? His brain was befuddled. An explanation could wait until he had time to think over what they'd just discussed. But…could she actually be telling the truth?

Greer appeared in the doorway. "I just saw Charlotte

running through the hall, crying. She didn't stop when I called to her. What happened?"

Niall thought fast. If there were one person in his family that might not think him completely barmy if he told the truth, it would be Greer. But Charlotte and he had agreed to a different story and they needed to stick to it. For now, anyway.

"I upset her by asking too many questions about her past." That was true, although it had nothing to do with being confined to an imaginary asylum somewhere.

Greer frowned at him. "Do ye think 'tis really our business?"

If Charlotte was from the future, yes…but… He shook his head. What was he thinking?

"I'm glad ye agree."

Niall blinked. Evidently, his sister had taken his head shake as an answer to her question rather than as a means of his trying to clear his thinking.

"Ye need to apologize and assure her we willna be prying anymore."

If it were only that simple. Niall sighed. "I will apologize, but ye ken Da and Simon willna be content to let the matter be."

Greer shrugged. "With the army coming to Inverness, Simon will be distracted and Da will be more interested in what the next plans are."

"That's true." According to Charlotte, that would be Fort George.

"Well, I'm going to go talk to Charlotte and tell her she doesna have to worry about us," Greer said.

Niall raised an eyebrow. "Just be careful ye doona ask questions yourself, sister."

She rolled her eyes at him.

After she left, Niall became thoughtful. While his father supported the Cause—or said he did—he had also said that the fighting would stay south. That victory would be had, once Stirling and Edinburgh were taken. Now that the army was coming north, Frasers would be involved in what came next. They had been training—nominally—but now it would be in earnest.

And, if what Charlotte said was true, it would be for naught.

Could she truly know the outcome? Fortune tellers at town faires might claim to know the future and some of the more wily even managed to gain a king's ear, but Charlotte made no claim to do that. She said she was *from* the future. How could it be possible?

People simply did not travel through Time. He reviewed the way they'd met. There had been nothing out of the ordinary on that night as he could recall. They'd marched around the foot of the castle, torches held high, followed by the ceremonial dousing them in the river. There had been a moment when the air became hazy from the smoke and the images of people shimmered, but then the air cleared and they had begun to dance. He'd noticed Charlotte, of course, and he'd made sure he was next to her when the group broke into two circles, but that was a normal, male reaction to a beautiful woman. Nothing otherworldly about that.

There were so many pieces of the puzzle still missing. Charlotte had admitted to him that she'd lied about the betrothal. She'd agreed to the new twist of escaping from confinement, but he doubted that was even close to the truth, considering he'd been the one who brought it up. He was also convinced, even if Simon and his father weren't, that she was not an English spy.

From every account Keir had given him, Charlotte had not often left the office. When she did, Keir trailed at a safe distance and reported she'd simply taken care of whatever business was at hand and had not met anyone.

Having eliminated those three possibilities brought Niall back to the present one that—against all odds and human logic—Charlotte was who she said she was. A woman from nearly 300 years into the future.

Contrary to what Greer had said, there was a question he would have to ask.

What did Charlotte mean when she said the Scots would meet defeat? If he knew that, perhaps he could change the outcome.

History, after all, was written by the victors.

****

For the next two weeks, Charlotte was caught in a whirlwind of activity. News that Prince Charlie was accompanying the Jacobite army to Inverness had everyone in a frenzy. Niall, along with Simon, left early in the mornings to ride out and recruit troops, and they spent the afternoons training them and drilling the regulars. She rarely had a chance to speak more than a few words to Niall in the evenings because he was surrounded by soldiers in the Great Hall, all of them eager to discuss the upcoming arrival.

She had caught him sending glances her way on several of those evenings, though, and knew a confrontation regarding how she'd left the other conversation was inevitable.

It came a few days later. It was a Saturday, which meant she wouldn't be going into Inverness to work, and she made her way to the Great Hall to break her fast in a more leisurely fashion than usual. She'd just finished eating when the door to the council room off the Great Hall opened and Niall emerged along with his father and brother and a couple of other men who had arrived yesterday ahead of the army.

Niall said something to Simon and then turned to approach her. "I'd like a word with ye."

The porridge she'd just swallowed felt like a lump of lead in her stomach and she hoped she wouldn't cast it up. She'd been dreading continuing the conversation because she was pretty sure he wouldn't believe her, and she didn't know how else to persuade him. Still, the conversation needed to be held.

"Of course."

She followed him back into the council room, a place she'd not entered before. In contrast to the study with its leather chairs, bookcases, and warm hearth, this room was spartan and could have served as a monk's cell, except for its size. A long rectangular table with a dozen straight-back wooden chairs were the only furniture aside from a smaller table in the corner, littered with maps.

Niall pulled out two chairs and turned them to face each other. He gestured to one. She sat, took a deep breath, and waited.

He studied her, took a deep breath himself, and came to the point. "Ye said in our last conversation that the Scots wouldna win this war. Why?"

The only way she could answer was bluntly. "From what I read, there was confusion among the leaders on how to proceed at Culloden."

His eyebrows rose. "At Culloden? That makes nae sense, particularly since Lord Culloden has already ordered Colonel Campbell to move their troops into

Sutherland ahead of Prince Charlie's force of thousands arriving. The English are already gone."

"So I heard." As soon as the words were out of her mouth, she regretted them. There was still suspicion that she might be relaying information to the colonel since they shared the same name. She shrugged. "It was all anyone could talk about."

Niall waved a hand dismissively. "Aye. It makes it easier for the prince's troops to lay siege to the fort, too. I doubt it will stand for long."

She nodded, grateful he didn't press the subject. "The major will surrender."

He knit his brows. "Did ye read that too?"

Was he being sarcastic? He didn't sound like it, but in any case, she might as well tell him what she knew. Maybe it would convince him—if he didn't think her some sort of witch—that she actually *knew* the future because she was *from* the future. She was going to have to risk it.

"What I read is that the Jacobite troops will burn Fort George. They'll do the same with Fort Augustus. They won't be as successful with Fort William, though. They'll abandon that siege."

He stared at her silently. She fought a moment of panic, wondering if she had gone too far with trying to convince him. Finally, he shook his head.

"Those mostly sound like victories to me, lass."

"I suppose they are."

"Then why would Prince Charlie's men be going to a boggy moor at Culloden?"

She strove to remember. War strategy was not her strong suit. "I think the Duke of Cumberland will be advancing along that way from Aberdeen."

Niall sat back and folded his arms. “He is in Edinburgh. Why go north?”

“I don’t know why.”

“It makes nae sense, lass. He’ll nae doubt winter in Edinburgh. If what ye said is true about the forts, we are growing stronger each day.”

“You may be, but history says the prince wanted to meet the Duke of Cumberland head-on even though his generals opposed the idea.” She hesitated, not wanting to sound like a traitor. “Prince Charlie wouldn’t listen.”

“Hmph. That does sound like something the prince would do.” He shook his head again. “’Tis a lot of information ye’ve given me, lass. I’ll have to think on it.”

“Will you believe me if what I’ve told you about the forts is true?”

He considered, then slowly inclined his head. “I doona think I will have any choice if things turn out as ye say.”

“Thank you! I hope…” She paused again. “I hope it’s possible to rewrite history and prevent the battle at Culloden from taking place.”

“And this battle is so important?”

“Yes. It will be Scotland’s final defeat.” She thought how to word the rest. “And it will be a massacre.”

He went quiet and she stayed silent too, giving him time to absorb the words. When he spoke, he was hardly audible.

“Do ye ken when this is supposed to happen?”

“Yes. April 16.”

Niall looked away, then up at the ceiling, then back to her. “Ye are sure?”

“That is the date in the history books.”

He turned contemplative, expressions flashing across his face until his features hardened like stone Finally, he nodded.

"Then we still have time."

Chapter Sixteen

With the prince's arrival, the entire town of Inverness was thrown into turmoil. The prince's whereabouts was a closely guarded secret, but the inns were filled with his officers. Thousands of soldiers sprawled in the fields, and the streets were filled at all hours of the day and night, the taverns staying open for as long as there were men wanting drink.

Not all of the men were disciplined, trained soldiers. Anyone willing to fight the English was welcome to join. There weren't enough women following the camp, either, which made the ones in Inverness vulnerable to men who wanted their needs satiated.

Niall didn't much like the idea of Charlotte going into Fergus' office each day with the army everywhere, and drove to her into Inverness himself each morning. He hadn't questioned Charlotte further about their conversation. At this point, time would tell if things came to pass as she said they would. Besides which, he was still trying to make logical sense out of what he still thought was impossible.

However, his sister didn't have any qualms about questioning *him*. Greer caught up with him one morning after he'd returned from Inverness. Seated across from him in the study, she didn't mince words.

"What have ye been hiding?"

"Hiding?"

"Doona play coy with me, brother." Greer studied him. "For the past week, ye have acted secretive."

"Secretive? I've been busy." Niall hoped to refocus her attention. "In case ye have nae noticed, we've a few thousand men about."

"Do ye think me daft? I practically trip over them." Her eyes narrowed. "'Tis nae what I mean, and ye ken it."

So much for that ruse. "I've been busy," he said again. "I've nae been hiding my activities."

"Aye, your activities. Ye take Charlotte into Inverness. Ye come home. Ye train. Ye eat. Ye train again. Ye go get Charlotte." She waved a hand. "'Tis nae what I'm asking. What is it ye are hiding?"

While his sister was not malicious in any way, she could be as tenacious as his brother and father. Even worse, she had an uncanny intuition at times, and this appeared to be one of them. He could hardly reveal his secret, though. Trying to explain that Charlotte had somehow arrived at the Hogmanay dance from the twenty-first century would make even his sister doubt his sanity.

Charlotte's predictions would come true—or not—soon enough. He contemplated the thought. Perhaps he could manipulate that information into something Greer might accept.

"I have been preoccupied by some of the strategies that I heard the prince was considering," he said. "I doona ken if he wants that information spread."

Greer made an exasperated huffing sound. "Ye doona want to tell me because I am a woman?"

Niall sighed. He should have known that was coming. "Nae, sister. 'Tis nae wise to let a commander's plans be heard by too many in case the wrong ears hear it."

She gave him a long look. "Do ye mean Charlotte?"

He started and then managed to restrain himself from laughing. If Greer only knew the irony of what she'd just said.

"Ye doona really think she is a spy, do ye?" his sister asked.

"Nae. I doona think that, but with so many strangers around—even some here at Castle Dounie, 'tis better to say nothing." He gave Greer a winsome smile. She didn't look convinced. "Doona be offended, sister. Keeping this secret has nae to do with the fact that ye are female."

"Then why can ye nae tell me? Do ye think I canna be trusted?"

A sudden image of a small terrier fiercely trying to dig a rabbit out of a hole passed through his mind, although Greer looked nothing like a terrier. She simply was acting like one. He sighed again as his sister folded her arms across her chest.

The door to the study opened just as he was about to share a bit of what Charlotte had told him.

"Sorry to bother the two of ye," Simon said, "but Major Grant has just surrendered Fort George. The army is setting fire to it."

Greer gave him a quick look. "Was that the secret ye didna want to share?"

He nodded, glad for the reprieve. "I didna ken exactly when it would happen, so I didn't want to take a chance on something going wrong because of me."

"Hmph." Greer rose and went to the door. "I suppose we'll have a celebration, then. I'd best go see to it."

Niall sat back as she left with his brother. So. The first of Charlotte's claims had come true.

****

"It does feel good to have something to celebrate, nae?" Greer asked Charlotte the next day as they sat in the solar making plans for a ceilidh. "We've finally got the English retreating and surrendering."

That was only temporary, Charlotte knew, but she didn't want to destroy Greer's hopes. And maybe—just maybe—now that she had told Niall what history had written, there might be a possibility of avoiding it. After all, Ray Bradbury had written about someone squashing a butterfly and changing the course of history forever. That story had been science-fiction, but why couldn't it happen in reality?

"I'm glad there were no casualties."

"Niall said it's because they decided to blow up the bastion facing the bridge instead of trying to attack the double layers of defense wall," Greer said.

Charlotte smiled. "I suppose waking up to an explosion and finding the main entrance missing might persuade the commander to surrender."

"Aye." Greer gave her an answering smile. "But Major Grant is a relative of ours, so I suspect Da might have something to do with it too."

Charlotte was surprised, given the reaction she'd gotten when she created her fictional betrothed Colin. "Your family is related to English Grants?"

"'Tis complicated," Greer answered. "Some clans are split between supporting the English and wanting a Stuart back on the throne. In our case, the major at the fort—George Grant—favors the English while another relative—James Grant—is a Jacobite."

“That must make for some tense family moments.”

Greer shrugged. “’Tis the same with the Duke of Atholl, who holds Blair Castle for the English. His brother is our General Murray.”

In reflection, it probably wasn’t so much different from the American Civil War where families split loyalties between the North and the South. She was about to compare that, but realized what century she was in. “I had no idea,” she said.

“Och, well. ’Tis the way it is.” Greer turned back to the list she’d been making for the party. “I’m just glad we’re finally going to have some fun. It’s been a long while since we’ve had a gathering.”

The ceilidh. Charlotte wished she could feel the same enthusiasm as Greer did.

Unfortunately, she had lost her zest for the event when Greer’s father mentioned that it was time he had the Gordons over for an evening and this would work out splendidly. She wasn’t sure what that meant, but uneasiness had stayed with her, especially since Fiona had visited the office about a week ago and Charlotte had overheard her father saying he was going to talk to Lord Fraser. Were Greer’s father and Fiona’s planning to make an announcement of a betrothal? Did Niall know about it? Would he have a choice, given that marriages were arranged in this century? Or…would he agree to it?

The thought sickened her. She knew she had no right to claim Niall’s affections, given the circumstances, but that didn’t stop her deepening feelings for him. When did emotions ever follow logic? If she wanted to be logical, Niall would no longer exist in her century. He would be ashes with a grave marker that she might visit. Tears welled up in her eyes at that thought. She must have made some sort of sound for Greer jerked her head up.

"What's wrong?" She put down the paper she'd been writing on. "Are ye crying?"

Charlotte swallowed hard and blinked rapidly to dissolve the tears. "No…I…just got something in my eye." For emphasis, she rubbed an eyelid. "A speck of dust, probably. I…I'm all right now." She took another fortifying breath, hoping she could control the horrible urge to weep.

"Ye look a little pale."

"I'm…fine. Really." Somehow, she managed to paste a smile on her face and gestured to the paper. "How far along in the plans are you?"

Greer gave her a doubtful look but didn't press the issue. "There will be a banquet in the Great Hall before the dancing and other festivities begin." She picked up the paper and frowned. "I'm trying to decide the seating arrangements on the dais. I doona want to offend any of the clan lairds that are attending, but I doona ken if we have room for all of them, especially since Da wants Mr. Gordon seated next to him."

Charlotte felt like she'd swallowed molten lead and just barely managed not to grip her stomach. "Do you…do you know why your father wants him there?"

"I am nae sure," Greer replied. "It could be that Da wants the other lairds to ken he has a solicitor at his hand to increase his power-hold now that the war has come to us." She grimaced. "'Twould be like Da to do that."

From what Charlotte had observed and heard about Greer's father, it might be a motive. The Frasers were the biggest—and possibly the most important—clan in this region. It would be natural in the alpha world for Lord Lovat to establish his dominance through such a subtle gesture that wouldn't give offense, but it offered Charlotte only a glimmer of hope.

She was very much afraid that the real intention was to announce a betrothal between Niall and Fiona.

****

Charlotte looked up at the dais as she walked into the Great Hall the evening of the ceilidh. Greer had managed to seat all the visiting lairds at the table. Lord Lovat sat directly in the middle, with Mr. Gordon to his right. At least, Fiona had not been given a place, which Charlotte had thought likely if an announcement was to be made. Then again, Niall wasn't seated at the head table either, since it was full.

She found him seated at the smaller round table nearby that the family often used and where Greer had told her she would be sitting this evening as well. Her heart dropped to her stomach when she saw Fiona already seated next to him. Simon was on his other side, so Charlotte took a seat between Greer and Keir across from the brothers and pretended not to notice when Fiona nudged her chair closer to Niall.

"'Tis excited I am about tonight," she said, her gaze on Niall. "I canna wait to dance."

"'Twill be a long night."

"I am looking forward to it." Fiona smiled at him, looking very much like a cat who'd just discovered the creamery door open.

"Well, before we dance, we have to eat. The venison smells wonderful," Greer said as she lifted the dome off the platter in the middle of the table. "Niall, will ye do the carving?"

"'Tis my job," Simon stood before Niall could reply and picked up the knife.

Charlotte was grateful the attention turned to food instead of a continuation of Fiona's flirtation. Niall had not seemed to notice the chair shift… or maybe he didn't mind. Charlotte pushed the thought away. She'd already spent too much time thinking and worrying, these past few days. If she'd been in the twenty-first century, she might merely have *asked* Niall what his future plans were. Then again, maybe not. It would have sounded like an ultimatum of sorts, and those usually turned out badly. Besides which, there was a certain amount of decorum she had to follow in this time period, even though Vi would have had conniptions and fits about unequal rights. Women's Lib wasn't going to happen here. However, she had employed a plotting device and made subtle inquiries about Fiona to Niall, each one geared to learning more about their past. His answers had been noncommittal, much like the one he'd just given. Men could be exceedingly frustrating at times.

"This does look good," Niall said as he passed a plate with several slices of meat to Fiona.

She didn't take it. Instead, she smiled at him. "Would ye mind filling the rest of it for me? 'Tis nae polite for me to reach."

Charlotte felt her appetite disappear as she watched Niall silently add mashed turnips, cooked carrots, and a thick slice of bread pudding to Fiona's plate and then set it down in front of her. He didn't seem to *mind,* but then, did he have a choice? Even though there were just the six of them at the table, he and Simon were still the hosts.

Keir quickly followed suit by asking Charlotte if he could fill her plate, and after a somewhat surprised look, Simon did the same for Greer. Charlotte just hoped she'd be able to keep a few bites down.

As dinner proceeded, she watched the interactions covertly. Fiona, it seemed, was a master player. The term normally referred to men—at least in her century—but many of the characteristics applied in this situation. Tonight, the girl was all smiles, reacting demurely to Niall's general comments and managing to brush her hand or arm against his every time one of them moved. Charlotte wouldn't have been too surprised if she'd asked Niall to cut her meat and feed her since she seemed to be practically helpless. Charlotte started to snort, but managed to turn it into a cough.

"Are ye all right?" Greer asked.

She nodded, feeling Niall's eyes on her and tried not to choke. "Something just went down the wrong way."

"Mayhap a sip of wine will help?" Keir handed her the goblet, his hand closing around hers to make sure she didn't spill it.

"Thank you." She took the cup and swallowed, forcing her throat to relax and returned to pretending to enjoy her meal. Conversation buzzed again around her, but she paid scant attention.

Fiona was anything but helpless. Nor was she in any way feeble-minded. She was playing a game this evening and Charlotte was pretty sure every move was calculated, much like every move in a chess game was, to get what she wanted.

She recalled quite clearly the warning Fiona had given her the day they'd gone to lunch: *Niall Fraser is mine*.

The message was clear then and it was clear now. The question was, did Niall know?

****

Niall didn't much like watching Keir offer Charlotte

her wine goblet as she coughed. He didn't miss that his friend's fingers lingered over hers a mite too long, either. He furrowed his brows. It had been bad enough that Keir filled her plate, but there wasn't much he could do about that, given that Fiona started it by asking him to do the same for her. As host, he could hardly refuse, although he wondered why she asked. The food was all in the center of the table.

Fiona certainly was acting strangely tonight. He avoided glancing at her because each time he did, she smiled brightly and asked him some inane question. That wasn't like her either. Keir's sister was not one to blether on about nothing. She usually had strong opinions and wasn't afraid to voice them. Tonight, though, she was agreeing with everything he said. A poke in his side interrupted his thoughts. He turned to Simon.

"What?"

His brother leaned closer and whispered. "Ye look like a thunderstorm about to roll in."

"I do nae…" He let his voice trail off as he realized he was frowning. Relaxing his brow, he gave Simon a tight smile. "It this better?"

"Och, aye. Now ye look like a snarling dog."

He straightened his mouth. "Fine."

Simon leaned back and gave him a curious look. "We are celebrating a victory, in case ye've forgotten."

"I've nae forgotten."

"'Tis talk of taking Fort Augustus next."

Niall was glad he'd already schooled his features and therefore managed not to show any emotion. The hair rising at his nape was another matter. It seemed another of Charlotte's predictions was going to come true. He glanced at her. Had she heard?

She had. She raised one eyebrow subtly as she met his gaze. He held the look until his brother cleared his throat and he realized what he was doing. Simon glanced from Charlotte to him and Niall knew he was trying to analyze the situation. He would have to be careful he gave nothing more away.

Fiona touched his arm. "The music is starting. Ye promised me the first dance."

He had done nothing of the sort. He'd intended to ask Charlotte. However, it might be best to acquiesce to throw his brother off the trail.

He pushed back his chair and stood. "My pleasure."

Simon stood too. "And I'd like to request the honor of dancing with our guest, Miss MacGregor."

A fleet of emotions passed over Charlotte's face so quickly, he couldn't read any of them. His own face felt like the thunderstorm really was rolling in this time. If his brother interrogated Charlotte, he would…

That thought didn't get finished because as Fiona stood she managed to press her breast against his arm before she turned. From her knowing smile and the way her tongue darted out at the corner of her mouth, it had been deliberate.

Suddenly, he realized why Fiona had been acting like she did. She was still interested in him. He glanced at Keir, but he was talking to Greer. He hoped his friend was right and that, by the time the night was over, Fiona would have found another man. Or…another man would find her.

He suddenly had a different goal to accomplish tonight.

****

"My pleasure," he said. It might have been a

socially benign response from Niall that had no further meaning. Or did he genuinely mean dancing with Fiona would be truly pleasurable and that he was looking forward to it?

The words echoed through her mind as she watched Fiona press herself against him as she stood. *Slithered* would have been a better word. Charlotte noticed that Niall gave a quick glance toward Keir, but she couldn't interpret it. Was he hoping Fiona's brother wouldn't notice? At least, they wouldn't be waltzing, since that dance had not yet reached Britain's shores.

Simon had his arm extended and she remembered now that he had asked her to dance. It was a rather strange request, since he'd remained aloof ever since she'd arrived at Castle Dounie. She placed her hand on his arm and forced a smile. He gave a curt nod in return, which led her to believe that he was trying to divert her attention from Niall and Fiona instead of wanting to dance with her. He probably agreed with his father that the match would be a good one.

Her suspicions were more or less confirmed when they lined up to dance a version of a reel that resembled the country-western square dances of rural Texas.

"Are ye interested in Niall?" he asked on the first pass.

That was certainly blunt enough. Thankfully, she had a spin and step to take before she came close enough to answer him.

"Your brother has been very kind to me."

"Nae the question I asked, lass," he replied as they separated again.

The rest of the dance was peppered with similar questions to which she managed to make noncommittal replies, but she was thankful when the dance ended. She turned to go back to the table when he caught her elbow.

"I think a bit of fresh air would be good."

"It's February."

"There's nae snow on the ground at the moment, so it will be tolerable." Simon gave her a direct look. "There's questions I want answered and I doona think ye want me to ask them here."

Charlotte glanced quickly around. Keir and Greer were at the far end of the room, not looking in her direction. She didn't see either Niall or Fiona anywhere. She narrowed her eyes slightly. Maybe *they* were outside enjoying a "bit of fresh air" and Simon wanted her to run into them. There had been no announcement made of a betrothal at the dinner, but if she saw them embracing or kissing, she would have her answer. Which is probably what Simon wanted. She sighed.

"All right, but I don't intend to stand out there for long."

"That will be up to ye."

He did stop long enough in the foyer to grab two cloaks from pegs and handed one of them to her. As she wrapped it around herself, Niall's familiar scent of heather soap and leather engulfed her. How ironic—and possibly cruel—that Simon had handed her Naill's cloak.

She followed him silently as he led the way around the corner of the castle to a hedged area that blocked both wind and view and had a folly. It would be a perfect place for a tryst, come summer, but even now it afforded the privacy for a kiss or two. She braced herself for what she would see once she got closer.

Surprisingly, though, Simon stopped and turned to

her.

Was Niall not here? Why would his brother have brought her out here if not to find Niall and Fiona in a compromising situation? Simon had asked endless questions during the dance, so she doubted he had more.

Uneasiness suddenly swept through her as she realized she was alone with a man in a dark, secluded area. She swallowed hard and started to step back, but he stayed her.

"Why…why did you bring me out here?" She tried to pull her arm away, but he held fast. "I'll scream if you don't let me go." Not that it would do any good, with the music going on inside. No matter. She raised her chin and glared at him. "I will scream."

His eyes widened as comprehension dawned on him. He dropped his hand and shook his head. "Ye can rest easy on that, lass. I am nae planning to hurt ye."

Well. He hadn't hurt her. His grip had just been firm. He wasn't making any move toward her, either. Still, she took a couple of steps back to put space between them so she could run if she needed to. He didn't move.

She glanced at the folly again, but it seemed empty. "Why are we out here?"

"I told ye. I have questions."

"I answered your questions during the dance."

"Ye *evaded* my questions." He shook his head again. "I am nae moonstruck by ye like Niall is, so I'll nae believe your lies."

"My lies? I—"

"Doona lie again. I grow weary of it."

A different kind of uneasiness settled over her. She pulled Niall's cloak tighter for comfort. "I don't know what else I can tell you."

"For starters, ye can tell me who ye really are and what ye are doing here."

Chapter Seventeen

Niall stepped out of the council room just in time to see Simon and Charlotte leave the Great Hall. Where were they going and what the hell was Simon thinking of doing? Niall forced himself to keep to a walk rather than stomping after them. He was already angry that Fiona had managed to dupe him into entering the council room on the pretense that her father wanted to talk to him privately about keeping Charlotte at the office. Like an eejit, he'd believed her, only to find the room empty.

Once outside, he caught a glimpse of them rounding the corner toward the hedged garden. He frowned. He knew Simon didn't believe her account of her past, but why would he be taking her there? Niall had never suspected that his brother had designs on her, although Simon had remarked on more than one occasion that she was quite bonnie. Maybe he thought he could lure her into the folly and seduce her to get the truth out of her. Or intimidate her into talking. He couldn't let that happen.

Niall burst into a run.

****

Charlotte was thinking hard on how to respond to Simon's question when she heard thundering footsteps and saw a flurry of movement rounding the corner of the castle.

"*Je suis prêt!*" a voice roared. "I am ready!"

A heavy thud followed the battle cry as Simon landed on the ground. In the scuffle that pursued, she heard growls and grunts and words in Gaelic that were no doubt curses as the men rolled over and over.

When the two finally disentangled themselves, she recognized Niall, although it took a moment. Everything about him was different. His stance was that of a Roman gladiator, feet wide apart, shoulders hunched, arms spread open. His hair was disheveled, sticking out wildly at all angles, and his eyes glinted like fire in the dim light. Rage rolled off him in waves. He looked like a wild beast…a Highlander unleashed.

Simon was bent over too, but mostly to catch his breath. He wiped his bloody nose as he straightened and glared at his brother. "Have ye gone daft?"

Niall didn't answer him. Instead, he turned to her. "Are ye all right?"

Charlotte blinked. Niall had attacked his brother because of her? She couldn't recall any man coming to her defense before, especially not in such a physical way.

Before she could answer, he swung his head around to Simon.

"If ye've hurt her, I willna be finished with ye."

"I havena." Simon took a wary step back and looked at Charlotte. "Tell him."

Still somewhat flummoxed, she nodded. "I…I'm fine. Really."

Niall didn't look entirely convinced, but at least he'd unclenched his fists and relaxed his shoulders. "Tell me true. I'll nae have ye besmirched."

Besmirched? Niall was defending her honor? Sweet Lord in heaven! She wrote about gallant heroes who came to their lady's defense, but she couldn't have written a better scenario than the one that just happened. Maybe Niall didn't have a white horse or shining armor, but she had just dubbed him her knight.

****

Her "knight" bore the remnants of last night's skirmish the next morning when he appeared at breakfast. He had a welt on his forehead and the knuckles of both hands were scraped. Simon had fared worse. Both of his eyes were blackened, the one nearly shut, and he had a split lip along with a bruise on his jaw.

Greer looked from one of them to the other. "Was there trouble last night that I didna hear about?"

Simon shook his head quickly. "No."

"Yes." Niall scowled at his brother.

Greer knit her brows. "Which is it?"

Charlotte studiously kept her eyes on her plate of eggs and sausage, hoping Greer wasn't going to question her next. After the altercation, Simon had stomped off, giving her a dire look that meant he still wanted an answer to his question. Niall had escorted her back inside without saying much. It didn't seem like a good time to tell him Simon wasn't going to back down since she could practically feel the anger still rolling off him. Once they got inside, he'd left her and didn't return. Since they were both sitting at the table now, the best thing to do was to stay silent and hope one of them would change the subject.

That hope didn't last long as Greer leaned over to touch her hand. "Do ye ken anything about this, Charlotte?"

"Well, I—"

"Niall and I had a misunderstanding over something," Simon told Greer. "'Tis nothing to concern yourself about."

"'Twas nae a misunderstanding," Niall countered.

Greer's eyes widened. "The two of ye fought each other?"

Simon glowered. "He attacked me."

"Ye deserved it."

"I didna do anything wrong."

"Ye did and ye ken it."

Simon shoved his chair away from the table. "Do ye want to finish it, then, brother?"

"If it will finish the matter, aye." Niall pushed back his chair too.

"Enough. Both of you." Greer landed a fist on the table for emphasis and then glanced at Charlotte. "I suspect they had a disagreement about ye, nae?"

She felt her cheeks flame. "It really—"

"—is nae your business, sister," Simon cut in. "Niall and I will handle it."

Greer was not about to be deterred. "Handle what?"

Neither Niall nor Simon answered. Instead, they glared at each other, each looking ready to spring at the other. Charlotte sighed.

"Simon does not believe I am who I say I am. He took me outside last night to talk."

Greer frowned at Simon. "We agreed to ask nae more questions."

"Ye and Niall agreed. I didna." Simon stared at Charlotte with his good eye. "I still want answers."

"Ye will just have to wait then," Greer said, "for we've more pressing matters."

"Like what?"

"A messenger arrived late last night. Da looked for both of ye, but couldn't find either of ye." She looked from one to the other. "Ye'd better come up with a good excuse for your bruises because Da is nae happy. His temper will worsen if he finds out ye were acting like lads in a schoolyard."

"Never mind that," Niall said. "What was so important about the message?"

"He didna let me read it." Greer grimaced in exasperation. "But he said the Duke of Cumberland is moving his troops to Aberdeen."

Charlotte looked down at her food once more, although she could feel Niall's penetrating look. She dared not return it in Simon's presence.

So far, the history books had been correct. It was not a positive thought.

****

Even though Charlotte had "predicted" it, Niall was surprised at how quickly Fort Augustus surrendered. A messenger from Colonel Stapleton's regiment had arrived a short time ago, and his father had summoned Simon and himself to the council room.

Their bruises had healed, although anger still lingered. It wasn't because they'd fought—they'd tussled often enough as boys and even young men—but this went deeper than physical assault. He sensed Simon no longer trusted him because he'd defended Charlotte. He could even understand that to a degree, but he could hardly tell Simon the truth. If it *was* the truth. His logical mind still had problems accepting travelling through Time, even if everything Charlotte had told him so far had come to fruition.

"What do ye think?" his father asked.

Thinking? His father wanted to know his thoughts? The notion quickly passed when he realized everyone was looking at him, waiting for an answer to some question he hadn't heard. "I guess I was woolgathering."

Simon gave him a sideways smirk, which Niall understood was an accusation that his woolgathering had been about Charlotte. True in its own way, but wrong implication. He hadn't been lusting after her. At least, not right now.

"Please repeat the question."

"It was more of an opinion we were asking for," the messenger said. "What do ye think of Major Wentworth being accused of surrendering too early and facing court-martial?"

He really hadn't been paying attention. "Too early? Hadn't the fort been under attack for a week?"

"Aye," the man answered. "It could have been destroyed earlier, what with the walls being weak and the bastions not square on the corners, but the colonel didna want to kill any more Englishmen than necessary since he was commanding French troops."

Considering that the French and English had been squabbling over claiming colonies in the New World, a situation that could easily escalate into open war at any time, the decision was probably wise. "It sounds to me like Colonel Stapleton was being lenient and Major Wentworth wise enough to see that."

"Wise?" Simon snorted. "Surrendering is what got him a court-martial."

"Under the circumstance, ye would have preferred to fight?" Niall asked.

"Aye. I do. Under the circumstances."

Niall was pretty sure the *circumstances* his brother was referring to weren't in regard to an English commander's decision but rather that their own in-house fighting hadn't ended with the brawl in the courtyard. He suppressed a sigh.

"Well," the messenger said, "we willna have to worry about who will be replacing Wentworth."

"Why is that?"

The man grinned. "As I was leaving, Scots were already setting fire to the place. There won't be any fort left to command."

Simon nodded. "Good news, that."

Niall didn't respond. So Charlotte had been right again. Fort Augustus was being burnt down. And if she were right about Fort William…

Well. Maybe *then* he could be more forthright with his brother about who Charlotte really was.

Chapter Eighteen

When Niall brought her to the Gordon's office on Monday morning, only Keir was there.

"Is your father ill?" Charlotte asked.

"Nae. He got called to Edinburgh on business over the weekend," he answered. "I'm just finishing a few things, and then I'll be closing the office for the week. Ye might as well go back home."

Charlotte looked at Niall. "Weren't you needing to go on to Dalcross today? Taking me back to Dounie will put you behind. The road is already muddy from last night's rain, so I'll slow you down."

He shrugged, then grinned. "Ye could come with me."

The idea of spending the whole day alone with Niall was definitely appealing. More than appealing. She knew in this century it would be totally improper, but then, *she* wasn't from this century. Still, she glanced at Keir, but he only shrugged.

"My lips are sealed if ye want to go." Then he smirked at Niall. "Or, I could take her home after I close up."

Niall frowned. "Charlotte is coming with me."

In the twenty-first century, Charlotte *might* have taken offense that the decision had been made for her. Vi certainly would. However, she rather liked the idea that Niall took the reins. He wanted her to spend the day with him. Who was she to argue?

"Let's be off, then."

They'd taken the wagon this morning since Niall needed to pick up supplies at Dalcross. That meant she got to share the driver's bench with him, which really meant that she'd be able to sidle up against him, since the wind had picked up.

"I hope ye willna be too cold." Niall spread a wool blanket over her lap. "'Tis nae much of a cover like the carriage would have been."

"The carriage would not have held the lumber you need. You didn't know you would be taking me along today, either."

He smiled. "'Tis a nice surprise. I'm nae complaining."

"Then…" She strove to keep a serious tone in her voice, just to tease him a bit. "…you won't mind if I snuggle up to keep warm?"

He blinked and then the smile widened into a grin. "Ye can snuggle as close as ye wish, lass." To emphasize his point, he put an arm around her shoulders and drew her close. "How's this?"

This was very nice. Charlotte tucked the blanket tighter over her legs and burrowed into the warmth of his embrace. She placed her arm around his waist, feeling the taut muscles go tighter. She was tempted to let her hand slip down a bit, but restrained herself. They were hardly out of town and it wasn't like they could just pull off the road for a bit of sport. Besides which—and maybe the eighteenth century was having an effect on her after all—she didn't want to throw herself at him, like Fiona had done. She gave herself an inward shake. She didn't want to think about Fiona, either. Especially not when she had the entire day to spend with Niall.

"I think I'll stay just like this the whole time." She frowned slightly. "That is, if you can drive with just one hand."

His hand tightened on her shoulder. "I'll manage, lass."

"Good." She burrowed closer and sniffed his welcoming scent. "You smell good." The words were out before she thought about it. Feeling him tense, she wondered if she might have sounded too provocative. This was really not the time. "Besides, you're warm," she added practically, hoping to ease the sudden tension. "I think it's getting colder."

"Aye." Niall squinted at the sky. "Most likely another storm brewing over the Forth."

Charlotte looked up too. The clouds were definitely thicker and darker. "Do you think we'll have another blizzard?" She wouldn't mind being stuck at an inn in Dalcross with Niall overnight, although she didn't voice that thought.

"I doona ken. Hopefully we'll get home in time."

Well. That put the pin in her balloon. Niall didn't want to spend the night with her? Maybe she had misinterpreted his defense of her when he'd bowled Simon over in the yard? Maybe he was only being chivalrous, after all? Maybe he really did like Fiona? She straightened.

"I think I'm warm enough now."

Niall gave her an odd look. "Are ye sure?"

"Yes. I'm fine."

He hesitated, searching her face, then slowly withdrew his arm and took the reins in both hands. "Tell me if ye get cold again."

"I will." She would *not*.

Niall gave her another odd look, then clicked the reins on the horse's back to urge it to a trot once they'd reached a smooth part of the road which wasn't rutted in mud. It just proved that he was eager to get business done and be on the way home.

The air grew much colder and Charlotte tried not to shiver. By the time they reached Dalcross, she was beginning to regret her determination not to embrace Niall's warmth once more.

He stopped in front of the inn. "A cup of hot cider will help ye thaw out," he said, as he helped her down from the bench. "Ye might get a bite, as well. I'll collect the things I need and come back to pick ye up in about an hour."

Cider did sound good—maybe she'd spike it with a bit of whisky—but the irony of walking into the inn with Niall for food—and not a room—made the all-too-familiar and frequent hysterical bubble rise. She squelched it. Obviously, she'd spent too much time writing historical romance novels. This was reality. Food. Beverage. Not bedding her hero.

"Don't leave without me." She'd meant that as a joke, but it came out sounding rather pathetic.

"Doona fash." He squeezed her elbow and let go. "I'll be back."

The writer in her wanted to find a reassuring double entendre in that, but it had only been a statement. She really needed to remember where she was.

An hour later, warmed by both soup and cider—the innkeeper had put a dram of whisky in it—the air didn't feel as cold when she stepped outside.

"It feels like it's a bit warmer. I guess that means no

blizzard."

Niall didn't answer right away. Instead, he searched the skies, then lifted head and sniffed much like a pointer dog would. "Snow's in the air."

That reminded her of the conversation she'd had with Thea and Vi at Hogmanay. Which seemed like centuries ago. She suppressed a giggle. Actually, it had been *centuries*…future ones. She shook her head to clear it. Maybe she'd had a bit too much whisky in the cider.

"You can smell snow?"

He shrugged. "In a way. It's the freshness in the air, like after a spring rain. Besides, with the wind dying, the clouds are thickening. "We'd best get started for home."

The reminder that he wanted to get home before a storm broke sobered her. "Of course. I'm ready." That came out wrong. "To go home, I mean."

He gave her that strange look again, although he stayed silent. By the time they'd gone a few miles, slowly this time since the horse was pulling a load, she began to feel sleepy and wished she hadn't added alcohol to her cider. The thought of snuggling against Niall again was becoming more and more enticing She struggled to keep her eyes open and sit upright. The sway of the wagon was making it hard to stay awake. Then she felt the sting of something on her cheek and her eyes sprang open. Another sting struck and then another. She looked up as tiny ice pellets rained down.

"Sleet?"

"Aye." His voice sounded grim. "Ye had best cover up with that blanket, lass."

The pellets were coming faster and heavier, feeling like sharp jabs with a needle. Charlotte shook out the blanket and covered both their heads with it and threw caution to the winds as she wound her arm around Niall's waist again and burrowed into his shoulder. She felt his arm go around her and she felt safe…and sleepy once more, now that she was cocooned in his embrace. They still had miles to go before they'd even reach Inverness. Maybe a nap wouldn't be such a bad thing…

She felt a sudden lunge and heard Niall curse as the world suddenly turned sideways. She was falling…floating…and then came a hard thud.

When she opened her eyes, she saw swirling whiteness and a dark object looming over her.

****

Niall took one look at the broken axle as he leapt from the bench, his main attention focused on Charlotte, who had been thrown to the ground when the wagon tipped. He prayed—even though he'd just cursed a second ago, God forgive him—that she wasn't badly hurt or even dead. It had been a sickening thud. As he started to kneel beside her, she opened her eyes. He breathed another prayer of thanks.

"Lie still until I can check to make sure nae bones are broken."

She blinked at him and he wasn't sure if she understood. He ran his fingers gently over her shoulders and arms, then moved aside her cloak so he could trace the outline of her ribs. Her eyes widened and she inhaled sharply.

"Does it hurt when I touch ye?"

She blinked again. He was beginning to worry that she'd had a concussion when she giggled. "It tickles."

If she could laugh, nothing was probably broken. Still. He wanted to make sure. He spanned the side of her hips and the outside of her thighs when she made a completely different noise, something between a moan and a squeal as she squirmed beneath his hands. He suddenly became very aware of where he was touching. His manhood hardened instantly, even as he dropped his hands. He fought to concentrate on something other than rapidly rising lust.

"Can ye wiggle your toes?"

"I think so…*ouch*!" The last came out as she'd swiveled her right foot.

"Doona move it more," he said, "if it's sprained or broken, your boot will act as support until I can get ye inside somewhere."

Charlotte raised herself to a sitting position and looked around. "Where would 'inside' be? What happened anyway? I fell asleep."

"The sleet froze the mud and one of the wheels got caught in a rut." Niall pointed to the wagon. "The axle broke and ye flew out when the wagon started to turn over."

She looked at the wagon leaning sideways on the road and then at Niall. "How far are we from home?"

He shook his head. "We are only halfway to Inverness."

She studied him. "What are we going to do?"

Niall didn't answer immediately. He looked up and down the road—or as much of it as he could see, since it had started snowing again. It was unlikely that anyone would be happening by in this weather. "I'll un-harness the horse and put ye on its back. Then we'll walk until I find a crofter. I think I remember seeing something nae too far back."

"They'll put us up?"

"Och, aye. 'Tis the Highland way nae to refuse a

traveler in bad weather." He stood. "I'll be right back."

Thankfully, his memory had served him correctly. It wasn't more than a mile before he sighted the building they'd passed before. Unfortunately, no one answered when he knocked. Trying the door, it opened easily. He peered around, then turned back to Charlotte.

"'Tis empty. Probably a sheepherder's cottage. He won't be back until spring."

"Can we use it?"

He considered his options. Dalcross was at least three or four miles away. With the leaden skies, darkness would come early and, this time of year, the storm could easily strengthen quickly. Inverness was even farther away in the other direction. He couldn't remember seeing any other crofters close to the road, but he hadn't exactly been paying attention to buildings this morning while Charlotte had been wrapped around him.

Now she was shivering so badly she was shaking. The horse shimmied beneath her when he felt the quivering and stamped a hoof.

"We can use it." He lifted her off the animal's back and carried her inside, setting her down on a straight-back chair that wobbled only a little. "Stay seated until I get the horse in the shed and taken care of. I'll try to find some dry firewood. When I return, I'll tend to your ankle." He walked to the door, then turned. "Remember. Doona move until I get back and can make sure ye doona have a broken bone somewhere that I missed."

****

He should have known she wouldn't listen. His sister never did.

A small fire was gathering strength in the hearth when he returned with a few semi-damp broken boards he'd unearthed. He noted there was a fire-bin in the corner that he hadn't seen. Not only that, but Charlotte had found a couple of quilts and laid those by the fire and was currently sitting on them. She'd removed both her boots and her cloak. She wiggled her toes.

"I don't think my ankle's broken."

"It doesna look like it." He removed his cloak and wet boots, setting them by the fire to dry before joining her on the makeshift rug. "Do ye think ye're hurt anywhere else?"

"I don't think so." She paused, then smiled at him slowly. "But you are welcome to…er…examine me again."

He stared at her, not quite sure he was interpreting correctly what she was saying. She gave him a tentative look. "That is, if you want to." Her smile faded. "I'll not ask again."

Heat shot straight to his groin. "Ye willna have to ask again, lass."

****

Charlotte sighed with relief. She'd had a moment of near panic that he might just refuse. She reached for the fastener on his breeches.

Niall grinned. "I can do this faster myself."

"I want to touch you."

His grin widened. "Ye'll have opportunity to touch me everywhere." He pulled his shirt over his head and tossed it aside, divesting himself of pants and socks so quickly Charlotte could only smile too.

Even though she knew Niall was muscular and strong, she'd never seen him naked. He was magnificent. The hard plateau of his chest was dusted with a sprinkling of hair that melded into a narrow downward trail. Broad shoulders sloped to well-defined biceps that bulged with his every move.

In another few seconds, her clothing was off too, and Niall lay down beside her. "I think I'll feast on ye first."

He nuzzled her neck, nipping at her earlobe, before trailing his tongue down the side of her throat and along her collarbone. Then, he slowly began circling her nipple, while his hand cupped her other breast, kneading it. He flicked his thumb lightly over the hardened peak, teasing it until she arched her back in pleasure.

"Please. More…"

He pulled back. "Mayhap I should make ye wait."

"No! Please! You don't know how much I've wanted to do this."

"Nae more than me," he said, drawing the nipple's tip between his fingers and pinching while his mouth covered the first one. Charlotte mewled softly when he began to suckle, the sound turning into a moan when he drew her nipple deep and tugged hard on the other one at the same time. A delicious tingle shot from her breasts directly to her core.

Niall turned his attention to the nipple that still throbbed pleasurably from being pulled. Cool air swept across the breast he'd just left as heat encompassed the other, causing another delightful jolt to course through her.

His hand traced along her ribs and across her stomach. He certainly wasn't checking for broken bones this time. Muscles clenched deep in her belly as he cupped her mound and his fingers parted her already slick folds to find her sensitive little nub. Charlotte whimpered as his thumb encircled it, pressing and flicking until her body started to quiver. She cried out in earnest as he inserted fingers into her sheath and continued to rub the pulsing bud with the flat of his hand. The friction nearly lifted her off the bed, and she exploded like a volcano.

Niall didn't wait for her to come back to earth. Instead, he pulled her thighs around his hip and slid into her fully and began to thrust. Feeling him enter and then fill her completely set off a second set of spasms and she screamed when he gave a final, hard thrust that pushed against her womb.

She wasn't sure how long it would take before she was capable of speaking, but maybe she didn't need to. Niall slipped off to the side of her, pulling her tight against him as he wrapped one of the blankets around them.

"I…that was…"

"I ken," he said and laid her head against his shoulder. "Sleep now."

****

The morning dawned frigidly cold. Sometime during the night the fire had died out, leaving actual icicles hanging from the frame of the doorway, which didn't seal properly. Even now, gusts of cold air swept through the room. As much as she would have loved to have another romp before they left, common sense dictated that putting on clothes—not leaving them off—was the priority. She was shivering so badly that she was shaking, in spite of Niall's warmth.

"'Tis nae wise to build a fire since we'll be leaving soon," Niall said. "I doona want ye catching the ague either."

"Then I suppose we need to get going," she replied, hating to release him.

Niall gave her a look she couldn't interpret, then leaned forward to brush a kiss across her lips before he sat up and reached for his breeches. "Aye, lass. The sooner we start for home, the better for both of us."

By twenty-first-century standards, there really wasn't any hurry, but here, in the 1700s, being found together after spending the night in an empty cottage would have dire consequences. He'd be honorable enough to propose marriage. The notion wasn't unwelcome, but the last thing she wanted to do was force him into a commitment that wasn't of his own making. Even if such situations worked in romance novels, reality was quite a different thing.

What she really wanted to do was discuss last night—how incredible it had been and were they going to continue—although men did seem to balk when a woman said she wanted to "talk." It would be wise to wait until they could be warm and comfortable and relaxed.

By the time she finished dressing, Niall had brought the horse around. "We'll have to send someone back for the wagon, since the wheel is broken, but at least we won't have to walk."

After only a half mile, Charlotte wasn't sure that walking might not have been a better idea. The gelding wasn't happy to be carrying two people, since he was essentially a carriage animal, and pranced sideways. Having no saddle—and not being a natural horsewoman—Charlotte kept slipping sideways in the opposite direction, even though she wrapped her arms tightly around Niall's waist. She pressed her face against his back for warmth, which limited her ability to talk. That was probably just as well, since he was concentrating on persuading the horse to follow his commands.

By the time they reached Inverness at midmorning, Charlotte was glad to slide off the horse. She ached, already feeling stiff, and was practically starving. After a quick breakfast of steaming porridge at a staging inn—which felt like a five-star hotel and restaurant at the moment—Niall rented a buggy to hitch the horse to and Charlotte gratefully, if not gracefully, climbed up on the bench and winced as she gingerly sat down.

Niall glanced at her. "Are ye sore?"

She assumed he meant from this morning and not last night. "I am not used to riding." Then she felt herself blush. On their second round of lovemaking, she had ridden him. Rather recklessly, at that. She glanced up at him, hoping he hadn't caught the double entendre. From his amused look, though, she was pretty sure he had. She felt her face heat again in spite of the cold. Perhaps they could "talk" this evening.

It didn't take long to reach Beauly after that. As they rode through the gate of the castle, Simon led his mount out, accompanied by several men.

"We were going to start searching for ye." He glanced at Charlotte, then back to Niall. "What happened?"

. Niall briefly explained what happened with the wagon, omitting the details of their overnight residence. Then he turned and helped Charlotte down. "I suspect ye will feel better after a hot bath," he said as she limped up the stairs to the entrance. "And then, later, we will talk, nae?"

She was glad he'd been the one to suggest it. She smiled. "I'm looking forward to doing both."

He opened the door and followed her inside. They had hardly gotten past the foyer when Fiona stepped out from the Great Hall.

"I was so worried about you," she gushed to Niall. "Your da was concerned too, especially as the night wore on."

"Were ye visiting last night and got caught in the storm?" Niall looked around, then back to her. "Is Keir here?"

"Aye, he's here." Fiona frowned. "We came over last night to drop off some paperwork for your da, and Keir slipped and fell on the ice as we were leaving, which spooked his horse and it stepped on him. The physician came out this morning and said he's got some fractured ribs. He'll need at least a week's rest before he can leave."

Something akin to a lead ball was settling in Charlotte's stomach. Mr. Gordon was in Edinburgh. Keir was out of commission. Where was Fiona planning to stay? The thought had barely formed when the answer came.

"Your da offered me a room to stay, so I'll be your guest." Fiona laid her hand on Niall's arm and smiled, not sparing Charlotte a glance. "Will it nae be wonderful to spend time together? We have so much to talk about."

Charlotte strove to keep her expression impassive. She and Niall had a lot to talk about too, but it didn't look like that was going to happen now.

Chapter Nineteen

It was going to be a long week. Niall managed to step back from Fiona on the pretense of removing his cloak. He cast a covert glance in Chalotte's direction, but she wasn't looking at him. Actually, she might have been a statue in the foyer for as still and rigid as she was standing.

"Your cloak?" he asked. "I'll hang it with mine while you go and enjoy your bath."

She turned then and studied him for what seemed like long, drawn-out minutes but was probably only a few seconds. Her expression was unreadable, but he had a feeling he was missing something. He just didn't know what it was.

"I see ye've finally arrived home." His father walked out of the Great Hall. "I was expecting ye back last night since we had guests for dinner. Did ye forget?"

He frowned. Forget? He didn't remember Keir saying anything about them coming over. Then again, maybe he had. He'd been thinking about spending a whole day alone with Charlotte.

Charlotte's chin lifted. "Excuse me. I need to get out of these damp clothes."

"Of course." Fiona smiled sweetly. "Ye would nae want to become ill."

Charlotte gave Niall a last glance before she turned and walked away. He was pretty sure he had just missed something else in that silent exchange.

"Well?" his father asked.

He reverted his attention. "The wagon broke an axle, so I was not able to return last night, but I didna realize a dinner invitation had been issued, either."

"Ye kenned I needed papers from Fergus and that Keir and Fiona would be asked to stay for dinner since he was away." His father waved a dismissive hand. "Nae matter now. Where did ye leave the wagon?"

"Near Inverness. We were lucky an inn had plenty of extra rooms," he added before his father or Fiona asked the inevitable question. The inn probably did have available rooms, so it wasn't exactly a lie. He wasn't about to sully Charlotte's reputation, nor did he want to put her in a position of a forced marriage to him. Not that he found the idea unappealing. He hadn't for quite a while, and especially after last night… He pushed the thought away, lest his manhood start to betray him. He and Charlotte needed to talk. He had no idea of how she felt about the future. Both theirs and…well, the *future*. Better stick to the subject at hand.

"I met Simon in the courtyard. He rode out with a few others to retrieve it."

"'Tis good. I'll leave ye to entertain Fiona then, since duty calls me."

Duty? Niall watched his father walk toward the study at the far end of the hallway. His father had no duty at the moment. Had he pawned Fiona off on him? The hair at his nape rose at that suspicion, which was pretty much confirmed when Fiona stepped up and put her hand on his arm again.

"Let's go into the parlor by the fire, shall we? 'Tis cozy in there."

"I need to change clothes first," he said as he stepped back once more. "Perhaps a little later." He bowed shortly, ignoring Fiona's pout, and managed to get away.

As he went up the stairs, he wondered what sort of plotting his father was really doing. This was all too coincidental for his comfort.

He really needed to talk to Charlotte, but he would have to be careful when and where he did. Very careful.

****

He had dismissed her. Charlotte managed to restrain herself from slamming her bedchamber door behind her. *Dismissed.* She paced the short length between the door and the window several times before she realized she was making herself dizzy. Oh, he had covered it well, asking to take her cloak while she went to get her bath. He had been telling her to leave. So he could be alone with Fiona?

A knock on the door interrupted her tumultuous thoughts. "Yes?"

The maid Erin opened the door and poked her head inside. "Are ye proper? The lads have brought hot water for your bath."

Proper? She certainly hadn't been proper last night, at all. Even now, upset as she was, tingles shot through her at the memory. But the maid was referring to whether she was clothed. Which she hadn't been last night… *Stop.*

"Yes. Come in."

Erin pushed back the dressing screen so the two men following her could fill the half-bath behind it. In a few minutes, the scent of lavender steaming off the water infused the air. Her mood lifted considerably as she settled on the small seat in the tub and let the heat sink into her bones.

Maybe Niall hadn't intended to dismiss her. Maybe he'd been trying to divert a confrontation. He *had* said they would talk later. That had sounded like a positive thing.

But she couldn't understand what was happening. Apart from the precariousness of her time-travelling—which she wasn't sure Niall really believed yet—she couldn't ignore the reality of the present situation. Fiona would be staying at the castle for a week. She had made her intentions known, both at the ceilidh and just a few minutes ago in the foyer. Niall's father has also made himself quite clear by asking Niall to entertain Fiona while she was here.

In truth, much as she loathed the idea, she couldn't blame the circumstances. A marriage between the Frasers and the Gordons could be beneficial, especially since both fathers apparently had already approved the match. She *knew*, from the research she'd done for her novels, that a large percentage of aristocratic marriages were arranged for benefit of power or wealth. That had been the case in medieval times and had carried on into the eighteenth and even the nineteenth centuries, at least.

The water had cooled, and without its enveloping fragrance, her confusion returned. Reluctantly, she stepped out of the tub and dried herself.

She was naught but a guest here. One whose future—she smiled grimly at the irony—wasn't at all certain. Would she remain permanently in the eighteenth century? She hadn't found any portal back, but she could not remain at Castle Dounie if Niall were to become betrothed. She couldn't. But then, where would she go?

She'd had this conversation with herself before, but

that was before…before last night happened. So far, no one else knew, so the obligatory "duty and honor" of a marriage proposal wasn't mandatory, nor would she accept one unless she knew it came from Niall's heart.

As she dressed to go downstairs, she wondered if her future—and Niall's—was going to be determined this week.

****

It seemed their future—or talks of it—were going to have to wait. By the time Charlotte returned to the Great Hall, a messenger had arrived with obviously important news. Niall's family, along with a number of men and Fiona, had gathered around the man. Charlotte went to Greer. "What is happening?"

"Blair Castle is under siege."

She didn't remember reading anything about this. Charlotte tried recalling her geography. She thought the castle was close to Pitlochry. "Isn't that pretty far south of here?"

"Aye, but 'tis a strategic location on one of the main roads to Inverness," Greer replied. "'Tis held by the English-supporting Duke of Atholl, James Murray."

"Murray?" Charlotte remembered a previous conversation. "The brother of General Murray?"

"Aye." Greer shrugged. "There are those who doona think Prince Charlie will win. A duke would lose not only his title but also his lands if he sided with him."

Politics were politics, it seemed, regardless of the century. Understandably, losing one's lands was a risk many wouldn't be willing to take. It wasn't really just a matter of honor to fight for the Jacobite Cause, either. An English king could disperse the entire clan if he chose, and Charlotte understood enough about Scottish culture to know that lairds—even if they had English titles—still owed their real loyalty to the preservation of their clan.

"Do you think General Murray would burn it?" she asked.

"I doona ken. The messenger said they fired at close range."

"Still. To destroy your own ancestral castle—"

"'Tis a strategy. The English canna return to what is nae there," Greer answered and shrugged again. "Robert the Bruce made sure he left no castle standing that he'd taken."

She'd heard of burning bridges to stop an army's advancement, and leveling forts made sense, but castles were homes. People's lives and histories were there. She sighed. Wars were still happening in the twentieth and twenty-first centuries, too. World wars, Vietnam, Afghanistan, Ukraine… Homes, schools, hospitals—entire cities—were reduced to rubble. The old adage of history repeating itself until humanity learned its lessons must be true.

And she knew how the Battle of Culloden was going to end.

****

Niall looked across the small crowd that had gathered around the messenger and spotted Charlotte talking to his sister. He wondered if she'd known about the siege. She hadn't mentioned it when she'd predicted the taking of the forts. From the look of confusion on her face, it didn't seem that she had. Or maybe the whole thing wasn't important enough to be put into history books.

He caught himself with a hitch of his breath. Did he really believe she was from the future? His thoughts were certainly leaning that way, even though his rational mind kept telling him it was impossible. Even more irrationally, his mind didn't seem to care. He just knew he didn't want to lose her. Ever.

That thought jolted him as well. He glanced covertly at Fiona, who stood not far away. He hadn't been successful at redirecting her attention at the ceilidh, even though her brother had thought that might happen. He had no desire to marry her, even though he realized it was what his father—and probably Fergus—were plotting. Mayhap he needed to talk to Keir, although he didn't want to bring up such a topic while his friend lay upstairs with broken ribs. He couldn't afford a direct confrontation with Fiona either, since he had no wish to start a private war between the families. What he needed was space.

A thought formed. The messenger had mentioned he would be going to Inverallochy to inform Charles Fraser of the siege. He could save the messenger the trouble by going to see his uncle himself. It would take him away from Beauly for a few days and he could avert a crisis.

He nearly grinned at his brilliant solution. Cowardly maybe, but brilliant.

****

From the smaller table near the dais, Charlotte looked around the Great Hall. It was nearly filled since the evening meal was about to be served, but she didn't see Niall anywhere. Fiona sat as a guest of honor at the high table with Niall's father. Charlotte couldn't ignore the fact that the placement might well signal that Fiona would soon be a member of the family. At least, Niall was not seated next to her. But where was he? She turned to Greer.

"I don't see Niall anywhere. Did he ride out to help Simon bring the wagon back?"

Greer shook her head. "Nae. After the messenger left, Niall went to see our uncle over at Inverallochy to give him the news."

"Where is that?"

"On the coast, north of Aberdeen."

For a moment, she panicked. "How far north?"

Greer shrugged. "About forty miles, I think. Why?"

The Duke of Cumberland would be in Aberdeen. She couldn't tell Greer that though. In this century that would be a good two days' ride, and she didn't remember anything about the English going farther north. Niall should be safe. "I was just wondering how long he'd be gone."

Greer grinned. "If he's smart, he'll stay away until Keir and Fiona leave."

Charlotte felt her face grow warm. Hopefully, the dim light would hide the blush. "Why do you say that?"

Her grin widened. "Ye doona have to act the innocent with me."

Now her face felt on fire. How would Greer know that they'd made love? She couldn't. Could she? "What…do you mean?"

This time, Greer rolled her eyes. "Faugh! When ye think no one is looking, the two of ye act like *eoin gaoil*."

"Like what?"

"Love birds."

"We don't!"

"Ye do."

Maybe she should let this conversation drop. At least, Greer didn't know quite how love-birdy they'd gotten. Perhaps, though, it was time to get her opinion on certain matters. "I'll admit that I am very fond of your brother."

Greer laughed. "Fond, is it? I suspect ye'd rather use another word. So would Niall."

Her face reheated. "What would that be?"

She shook her head. "Ye'll have to get him to say it." She glanced at the dais. "But that one is going to be trouble. Ye'll have to be careful." She paused. "Ye ken?"

So what she suspected was true. Fiona's sights were set firmly on Niall. That he'd escaped her clutches for now was a good sign, but could he stand against both his father and hers?

"I do."

Or—regardless of what Greer thought—was it her own clutches Niall was avoiding?

Chapter Twenty

"Tell me what 'tis like in your world."

Charlotte blinked at Niall. They were in the council room again, this time with Greer. He'd come back late last night after having been gone nearly ten days. Fiona's father had returned from Edinburgh and Keir's ribs had healed well enough for him to go home. Confrontation had been avoided, although Charlotte wasn't sure if that was why Niall had been gone so long.

"My world?" she asked cautiously, glancing at Greer. It was a question she'd not been expecting, least of all in front of someone else.

Greer smiled. "Niall told me late last eve that ye are from the future."

She said it as matter-of-factly as though she'd been commenting on weather conditions. Charlotte turned back to Niall. "You believe me, then?"

"I doona think I have any choice, lass. Everything ye said has come to pass. The siege at Fort William was abandoned, as ye said it would be. Ye could nae have kenned all of these things otherwise."

He finally believed her! The relief was enormous. Her first impulse was to throw her arms around him and kiss him until they were both breathless. She remembered Greer's presence just in time and turned to her.

"Do you believe me too?"

Greer tilted her head to one side. "I'll admit I thought Niall had gone completely daft, but he said he needed someone to confirm he wasna barmy. That what seemed impossible might not be."

"Greer is the only one I could trust," Niall said. "I hope ye understand."

Charlotte nodded slowly. "I…do."

Greer straightened. "When he told me everything that ye'd predicted, things began to add up. Your sudden appearance with nae coin nor clothes. The 'friends' ye made up—"

"I didn't make them up. Thea and Vi are real…" She hesitated. "…at least they were—*are*—in the twenty-first century."

"Nearly three hundred years," Greer said softly. "What is it like?"

How to explain automobiles and airplanes, smart phones and the Internet? "There are so many things that would seem like magic," she answered. "I'll be glad to try and explain them, but it would take hours and hours."

"Later then," Greer replied. "Maybe tonight after Da and Simon have gone to bed and we can talk as long as we want to?"

Charlotte nodded. "I would like to do that."

"Do ye have family ye left behind? Children?" Niall gave her a direct look. "A husband?"

Although he was looking at her steadily, she thought she saw a little bit of wariness in his eyes. After all the lies she'd told, she hoped he would believe her now.

She returned his look. "No husband and no children. I have never been married." Something sparked in his eyes and disappeared. Relief? Or was it wishful thinking on her part?

"Ye have nae family, then?"

Was he wanting to know if she'd miss not returning to her own time? Not that it was exactly an option, since she'd found no portal. Still, if he were hoping she could be happy here… The thought sent a little tingle through her. She needed to be completely honest, though.

"I have family. My parents retired in Hawaii. I have a brother who lives in Colorado and a sister in California. I live in Texas." As the words were spoken, she wondered if they even knew she'd disappeared. They probably thought she was still doing research for her next novel.

Niall and Greer looked at her blankly and she realized the places she'd mentioned were not yet known. "They all became states after the Revolution."

"Revolution?" Greer asked.

Good lord. They didn't know about the Revolution either. She almost smiled. "Yes. In 1776, the colonists decided they'd had enough of English rule too. We rebelled and…" She let her voice trail away, remembering that Scotland would have a different outcome.

"…and you won," Niall finished.

She nodded reluctantly. "We did. We're independent now."

He thought that over and then sighed. "Prince Charlie has called for all troops to come to Inverness. And Cumberland has mustered his men." He paused. "I saw the front lines on the road as I neared Aberdeen. They are coming."

Silence filled the room. Charlotte tried to gather her thoughts as she looked from Niall to Greer and back.

"If you want to save your country, Prince Charlie

must be stopped from going to Culloden Moor."

****

"Ye have given me much to think about," Niall told Charlotte the next morning as they rode into Inverness. It was an understatement. He'd not gotten any sleep mulling everything over.

Charlotte nodded. "It must all seem like fantasy to you."

"But one I would like to share."

She gave him a startled look. "Truly?"

"Och, lass. To visit the future? Who could ask for more?" He glanced at her. "Has it been hard for ye here, adjusting to this time?"

"Not really." She lifted one shoulder, then let it drop. "The hardest part was convincing myself that I hadn't lost my mind. That this was real."

"Would ye go back if ye could?"

"I…I don't know."

'Ye would be content to remain here?"

"I…think…that depends."

"On what?"

She took a deep breath. "On you, I suppose."

"What do ye mean?" When she hesitated, then chewed her lip and looked away, he pulled the horse to a stop. "Tell me what is troubling ye." She took another deep breath, and he noticed her hands were trembling before she folded them tightly over each other. Then she lifted her chin and looked at him.

"Are you going to marry Fiona?"

He felt his eyes widen. He hadn't expected that question, but perhaps he should have, given the way Fiona had acted. "Nae."

Her eyes searched his face. "Even if your father and

hers want the match?"

"I will choose whom I take to wife."

"And they'll let you? There won't be repercussions?"

He shrugged. "I'll nae deny that my father has wanted the marriage. Fergus Gordon is one of the best solicitors in Scotland. He has connections in Parliament. To have Fiona as a daughter-in-law would be beneficial to my father. Much like he does everything else for his benefit."

She chewed her lip again. "If Mr. Gordon is that powerful, can he make trouble for you or your family if you don't marry Fiona?"

"I doona think he would." He shrugged again. "Even he did, 'tis nae his decision or my da's. The decision is mine." He picked up Charlotte's hand and, this time, it was his that was trembling as he pressed it to his heart. "'Tis ye I love, lass. Nae other."

Her eyes rounded like saucers and then she threw herself against him with enough force that the buggy rocked and the horse danced in its brace. "I love you, too!"

And then, there were no more words spoken as their kisses became heated and nearly savage in intensity. He slipped his hands under her cloak, allowing his thumbs to caress the sides of her breasts before sliding down to cup her arse and pull her onto his lap, where his manhood was already hard and throbbing. It was all Niall could do not to tear at their clothing, even though they were in the middle of a busy road and April was still chilly. He suspected they were radiating enough heat to start a fire with wet wood.

Loud cheering and clapping finally penetrated his

senses, and he broke the kissing to look up and see a number of passersby had stopped and were evidently enjoying the show he and Charlotte had been putting on. Carefully, he withdrew his hands and set her back on the bench.

"Pay them nae mind," he whispered as he picked up the reins and snapped the leads. "We'll be gone from here in no time."

To his surprise, she laughed and then turned to the crowd and waved before turning back to him. "I don't mind at all."

He grinned. "Are ye going to be full of surprises like this?"

She grinned back. "I'll do my best to try."

****

"Will ye sit down and stop prowling like a fox near a chicken coop?" Niall's father gestured toward a seat in the council room. "We've got business to discuss."

They certainly did. Niall yanked the chair out and straddled it, much too tense to sit still. His uncle Charles had just returned from a meeting with General Murray and the prince. The news was not good.

"So Prince Charlie is nae willing to listen to reason?" he asked.

His uncle looked a bit uncomfortable. "Let's just say he doesna agree with the general on strategy."

"Murray has the right of it," Niall said. "Guerilla tactics helped Robert the Bruce win three hundred fifty years ago. We have nae the cannons nor cavalry that the English do, but we ken the terrain and we ken how to use it to our advantage."

"Be that as it may, the prince dinna agree," his uncle answered.

"At least," Niall continued to argue, "he could have heeded the advice to hold our line on the ridge by Dalcross. We would have the advantage of the hill."

"Aye, but Prince Charlie wants to meet the English head-on."

'On an open field." When Niall had first heard his uncle mention Drummossie Moor at Culloden, his blood had run cold. Events were taking shape exactly as Charlotte had told him they would.

"Colonel O'Sullivan convinced the prince a Highland Charge would be more effective if there was running room."

Niall snorted. "The man's *Irish*. What does he ken about a Highland Charge?"

"The Irish have been good fighters thus far," Simon commented. "The prince wouldna want to antagonize them."

"Besides," their uncle added, "Prince Charlie also thinks more French forces will still arrive in time to aid us."

From what Charlotte had told him, King Louis wasn't sending any more troops. To hold out that hope when only a few days remained before Cumberland would reach Nairn was foolishness. With a sigh, Niall turned to his father. "What do ye think of the matter?"

"We all ken how stubborn Charlie can be." He shrugged. "Besides, 'tis hard to deny a prince."

"Does that mean ye'll follow him blindly?"

"I may nae be here," his father said. "I'm planning to ride out tomorrow to gather our far-flung relatives and bring them back here."

He was not particularly surprised to hear of his father's plans, although this was the first he'd heard of it. Speaking of foxes, his father was clever at evading danger. Niall turned to Simon.

"Will ye be leading the Frasers, then?"

"Simon will follow with a secondary regiment," his uncle said. "I'll lead the first group since most of those will be men that came with me."

So their own men would be behind the Inverallochy Frasers, not in the lead. Charlotte hadn't mentioned that, but it might not have been a fact that was ever written about. Although it would matter little once the actual battle engaged, he would let her think it offered a little protection. She had been as taut as a harp string the past few days, trying to think of ways to avert disaster.

"Do ye ken what Prince Charlie's actual plan is?"

His uncle nodded. "The prince plans to assemble our forces on the moor early on April 15 and await Cumberland to arrive."

"The 15th? Are ye sure?"

"Aye." His uncle gave him a puzzled look. "Why?"

"Ah…well, 'tis only two days away."

"We're as ready as we will ever be."

Niall didn't answer, but simply nodded. If the prince had chosen the fifteenth and not the sixteenth, as Charlotte said was the date given in the history books, maybe Fate was intervening and the battle would take a different direction.

He would pray.

Chapter Twenty-One

Charlotte watched from the battlements as Niall and Simon rode off with their uncle Charles to join the rest of the prince's army, which had amassed just outside of Inverness. From her perch above them, she could see the white silk scarf she'd given Niall as a token—maybe it was the romance novelist in her, but if her "knight" were riding into battle, she wanted to have him wear his lady's token—and, she secretly hoped, it would protect him since she'd said prayers over it. It fluttered now in the breeze.

Even though she knew that today, according to the history books, was not going to determine Scotland's fate—that would be tomorrow, April 16th—she was sorely tempted to follow them anyway. Beside her, Greer looked as worried as she felt.

"Ye are sure of the dates?" she asked.

"As sure as I can be." She said a silent, short prayer that the writers hadn't gotten it wrong. Which, she supposed, was somewhat ironic since she was still holding out hope that the actual battle *could* be prevented and history *would* be changed.

"Tell me again what's supposed to happen today."

Charlotte knew that Greer was seeking reassurance that her brothers and uncle would be safe, at least for today. Her friend wasn't questioning the facts, which was another irony in itself. Once Greer had been taken into their confidence, she had seemed relieved that there was a—somewhat—logical explanation to Charlotte's presence, even if the possibility of time-travel was still mystifying.

"According to the books, Prince Charlie is going to march to Culloden, line up his troops on Drummossie Moor, and wait for Cumberland to come."

"I suppose it makes sense to be prepared and ready." Greer gave her a doubtful look. "But ye said the duke won't be coming, aye?"

Charlotte nodded. "Today is the duke's birthday and he's supposedly celebrating at Nairn."

"Celebrating." Greer uttered a curse in Gaelic. "The duke is nae concerned about an upcoming battle in which men are going to be killed."

Charlotte closed her eyes. She hadn't told Greer that it would be a massacre and just how many Scots would die. Nor that the Duke of Cumberland would acquire the moniker of The Butcher because he'd give no quarter. That was something that didn't need to be said, especially if a miracle occurred and it didn't happen. She opened her eyes and sighed.

"Niall knows and he told his uncle. Maybe when they meet the prince, they can convince him to wait a day."

"This close to the final clash, I doona think Prince Charlie will be deterred." Greer shook her head. "He has never been known for his patience."

Nor for listening to wise council, Charlotte thought, but didn't voice that either. She didn't want to jinx the possibility of maybe—just maybe—the prince would take advice for once. History was more like a flowing river then a ridge of rocks. It would only take one small event—just like Ray Bradbury's butterfly story—to alter the course of history. It could be done. It could.

Still, she wasn't surprised when, as the sun was setting, a messenger arrived from Niall. Cumberland hadn't shown and Prince Charlie had ordered the army to march to Nairn and surprise Cumberland with a dawn raid on his camp.

Her heart sank to the bottom of her stomach. That part of history was accurate too. Only the army wouldn't make it by dawn and would have to retreat before the English saw them coming. Charlotte crumbled the note. It seemed that the battle at Culloden was going to take place after all.

And she was going to be there.

****

Having sent Simon off with most of the Beauly men to find food for them, Niall and his uncle approached the tent that served as a makeshift headquarters for the prince. He'd persuaded his uncle—after last night's debacle of marching over ten miles only to have to turn back the same ten miles—that making a final attempt to change the prince's mind about standing his ground here was worth the effort.

Unfortunately, a full-scale argument was in progress.

"Clan Donald has always had the right flank!" the laird, Alex MacDonald, nearly shouted.

General Murray glared at him. "My men are better trained and ye ken it."

"Much as I hate to agree, Murray is correct," General Dummond said to Alex. "Ye can join my forces on the left. "'Twill be important for the left to keep the redcoats from spreading out."

MacDonald shook his head. "'Tis my clan whose lands were ravaged and destroyed by Cumberland—"

"*Enough.*" Prince Charlie held up his hand. "I concur with Murray. And Clan Chattan…" He looked at Alex MacGillivray. "Clan Chattan will be in charge of the first center line, followed by Colonel Stuart's brigade."

If the situation hadn't been so dire, Niall would have been impressed by the amount of power and authority that was gathered inside the tent. Given that he had no rank and his uncle was a mere lord, he wondered if they'd even listen. On the other hand, they all had wiser heads than the prince, so maybe, if they saw reason, they could persuade Prince Charlie. He needed to try.

"Permission to speak," he said when the other men had quieted down.

The prince looked at his tartan. "Lovat, is it?" He waved a hand. "Permission granted."

"My uncle and I have just come in from surveying the troops," Niall said. "They are tired from nae sleep, exhausted from hiking twenty miles, and they're hungry. Half of them have gone in search of food or of shelter from the snow moving in." He paused and looked around, hoping he wouldn't see disdain on the officers' faces since such hardships were nothing new for soldiers. Their expressions were neutral, though. He took a deep breath. "I think our chances of defeating the English would be better if we continued it on another day."

"You expect us to retreat?" the prince asked.

"Temporarily," he replied carefully, "until the men have time to recuperate."

Murray tilted his head. "'Tis something to consider. We could go back to Dalcross—"

"Ye've always wanted to fight on that ridge," Colonel O'Sullivan interrupted. "We had this conversation before."

"It makes sense to take the higher ground," Murray argued, "and have them come to us."

O'Sullivan shook his head stubbornly. "On the moor, we have room for the Highland Charge."

"Aye, there is an advantage to going on offense rather than defense," Drummond put in.

Niall gave his uncle a desperate look. They were getting entangled in war strategy, which was totally missing his point. His uncle cleared his throat loudly.

"Gentlemen. Your Highness. Perhaps if ye allowed the troops to disperse for today, ye will have time to come to an agreement for tomorrow."

"Cumberland will make camp if he doesna see the Jacobite army on the moor." Niall looked at the prince, hating to faun, but desperate to prevent this battle from happening today. "Ye could then put into play your idea of surprising them at dawn."

The prince eyed him with more acumen than Niall had given him credit for. Slowly, he nodded. "I rather like the idea—"

"Your Highness!" A soldier burst through the tent's fold. "The English are on the edge of the moor!"

****

Charlotte stopped the buggy a good quarter mile from the battlefield. The last thing she needed was to be seen and sent back to the castle. She'd had a dickens of a time trying to persuade the stable lad that she had an important errand in Inverness that couldn't wait. When she'd finally gotten him to hitch up the horse, he'd gallantly offered to drive her in himself. She'd spent more precious time—she had more than just the five miles to Inverness to cover—convincing him that she would be fine, there were no brigands on the road this early in the morning and she was used to handling the buggy. That was partially true since Niall had let her handle the reins on occasion and the horse was not temperamental. In any event, it didn't matter. She had to get to Culloden.

She pulled her cloak closer as she started to walk. The wind had picked up, blowing drifts of snow from yesterday. The cold drizzle that had been falling this morning was turning to sleet. Miserable conditions for soldiers on foot, but maybe not ideal for cavalry either.

The sound of cannon made her jump. When the second one went off, she started running. She rushed past some boulders and then skidded to a stop at the edge of the moor.

The English formed a solid line on the far edge, their infantry in the middle and the dragoons along each edge. A solid sea of red was packed behind the front line, stretching back as far as she could see. They were not moving, but they were firing their guns.

On the Scots side, a terrific roar went up and the men in the center started sprinting forward in a charge. To the left, some men were not moving and others appeared unsure what to do. To the right, those soldiers had joined the charge only to collide with the center which had suddenly veered into them. Chaos quickly ensued, men milling about as orders from different directions were shouted.

Charlotte watched in horror as the English took advantage and moved forward, their guns and horses quickly encircling and overpowering the Scots whose charge had been bungled.

History was playing itself out in front of her just as it had been written.

She searched the field for Niall and finally spotted the tartans of the Frasers off to the right. She caught sight of the white scarf she'd given him. He was still on his feet and still fighting, even though the ground around him was littered with the wounded. And then his head snapped back as he clutched his shoulder and fell.

Charlotte tried to race forward, but her feet felt leaden and she couldn't move, as much as she willed herself to. She was living the nightmare that had haunted her. She couldn't run. Only this was *real*. She had to get to Niall.

Then, suddenly, there was quiet. No shouts, no cries of dying men, no trampling of horses' hooves nor clashing of swords. Time was standing still.

Her limbs loosened and she found herself moving amongst soldiers who stood still as statues. Reaching Niall, she knelt beside him. The white scarf was covered in blood. She quickly felt for a pulse and found none. Niall was…gone? He couldn't be! Not after—

"Doona fash."

Charlotte stilled. Where had those words come from? Nothing was moving and all was quiet save for that voice. Slowly, she looked up.

The auburn-haired woman she'd seen by the river—Bridgid—stood beside her. Charlotte blinked. "What…what are you doing here?" She shook her head. "Never mind. Can you help me?"

"Aye. I brought ye here. Now ye will return." The woman lifted both arms high. "*Gum faigh thu sith, Taibhse à Culloden.*"

"What…what does that mean?"

Bridgid smiled. "May ye find peace, Ghost of Culloden."

And then, white mist swirled around her.

Epilogue

Texas, present day

Charlotte knew the exact moment Niall gained consciousness, even though he didn't stir, lying beside her in her bed. She propped herself up on one elbow and waited.

Slowly, Niall's eyes opened. His head didn't move as he looked around. Luckily, her room was simply furnished with an oak four-poster bed, side tables, and dresser with mirror. Her walls were a muted beige, the bedspread and curtains hunter green. It wasn't all that much different from Castle Dounie.

His gaze found hers. "Is this heaven, then?"

"Not quite." She smiled. "You're in the twenty-first century."

"How did that happen? I remember being shot and then…nothing." He frowned. "I didn't die?"

"That's up for debate. When I found you, there was a lot of blood, and I didn't feel a pulse." She took a deep breath. "Are you ready for me to tell you what happened?"

"As much as I'll ever be." He propped himself up against the headboard, looked around the room once more and took a deep breath himself. "Tell me."

"I guess I really need to begin somewhat before the battle. Do you remember when you brought me to

Inverness and left me for an hour to talk to Mr. Gordon?" When he nodded, she continued. "Well, I was sitting on the bench, contemplating how I'd gotten to your world, when a young lady joined me—"

"I saw her." Niall looked uncomfortable suddenly. "We were watching to see if ye'd meet with a messenger."

Charlotte drew her brows together, then cleared her expression. "Ah. You still thought I was a spy at that point."

"Aye. 'Tis sorry I am."

She waved her hand in dismissal. "Not important now. The woman is, though. She told me her name was Bridgid.'

He looked confused. "Why is that important?"

Charlotte studied him before answering. "Because she was the one who brought me to you and sent us back here."

"*What*? Ye are nae making sense, lass."

"I know it sounds strange." She took a deep breath. "But the whole time-travel thing seemed impossible, yet it happened."

He inclined his head. "Go on."

"The whole thing came together once I—*we*—were drifting through the mist." She raised a hand to stop him from questioning. "It was the same mist I went through before I woke up in your century." Charlotte turned to Niall. "And then I remembered—while my friends and I were at the Hogmanay festival, an auburn-haired woman led the torch procession before we danced. She must have been the same person who spoke to me on the bench in Inverness, and she was the same person who appeared on the battlefield after you'd been wounded." She paused. “I don’t know who she is, but she had the power to take us through Time.”

“I think I ken.” Niall looked as though he was collecting his thoughts. “This will sound farfetched, but given what’s happened, mayhap…”

“Please continue.”

“Well, ye ken the festival of Hogmanay goes back to the Norsemen, and before them the ancient Celts, nae?”

“Yes.”

“Bridgid was a Celtic goddess.” He looked pensive. “She was most known as a fertility goddess, but she was also said to be able to divine the future.”

Charlotte felt her eyes round. “And, with the future, also Time?”

Niall nodded slowly. “It makes as much sense as anything else.”

“I think you’re right.” Charlotte felt the bubble rising again. “But no one is going to believe us.”

“Then we willna tell anyone,” Niall answered.

“True.” Her romance-author mind was beginning to awaken. “I can say we met while I was on my vacation to Scotland, and we fell in love and couldn’t bear to be apart…” She stopped. “Sorry. I shouldn’t assume that you—”

“’Tis the truth, lass. I loved ye in my time and I will in yours. ’Tis the reason Bridgid intervened, I think.” He paused. “I wish Greer could have come too.”

“I think if she’s meant to be in this century, Bridgid will send her.”

“If and when the time is right, I suppose.” A look of sadness momentarily crossed his face and then he shook his head and smiled. “But I am here and I am looking forward to discovering this new world, with ye."

Charlotte smiled too. "I'll be glad to take you on that journey, but first…" She put her arms around his neck and lifted her face for a kiss. "I want to make sure you are real and not a ghost of Culloden."

He grinned, "I think I can assure ye of that." And then his mouth covered hers as they sank beneath the covers together.

Afterword

Simon Fraser, 11th Lord Lovat, also known as "The Fox," was noted for his many feuds and changes of alliances as it suited him. After Culloden, he was arrested, convicted of treason, and executed by beheading in the Tower of London on April 9, 1747, at the age of eighty.

His son, Master Simon Fraser, was imprisoned at Edinburgh Castle 1746-1747 and remained in Glasgow "at the King's pleasure." He studied law at Glasgow University and received a full pardon in 1750. After that, he raised eight hundred troops for the English and was commissioned as a Lieutenant Colonel of the 78th Regiment, which was renamed the Fraser Highlanders. He fought during the Seven Years War against the French and helped capture Montreal during the Battle of the Plains of Abraham in 1759.

On returning to Britain, he became the 19th Chief of Lovat and was elected unopposed to the House of Commons where he was re-elected three times before his death in 1782 at age fifty-six.

A word about the author...

Cynthia Breeding lives on the Gulf Coast of Texas with a very non-spoiled poodle-mix and enjoys walking and horseback-riding on the beach, as well as sailing.

www.cynthiabreeding.com

Thank you for purchasing
this publication of The Wild Rose Press, Inc.

For questions or more information
contact us at
info@thewildrosepress.com.

The Wild Rose Press, Inc.